Books by Paul Volponi

Black and White

Hurricane Song

Rooftop

Rucker Park Setup

CRACK!

The fat kid had slammed me in the side of the head with that bat, and a lightning bolt of pain shot through me.

I could feel the warm blood on my face. It tasted bitter as it dripped into my mouth. For a few seconds I was seeing double, and there were six of them instead of three.

"You wanna steal from white people, huh?" screamed the tall kid with the goatee, trying to take the sneakers off my feet. "See how *you* like it!"

My legs started pedaling on instinct, like I was on a ten-speed, fighting him off.

"Give 'em over!" barked the fat kid through his clenched teeth, cocking the bat again.

I brought my arms up to protect my skull.

response

PAUL
VOLPONI

speak
An Imprint of Penguin Group (USA) Inc.

SPEAK
Published by the Penguin Group
Penguin Group (USA) Inc., 345 Hudson Street, New York, New York 10014, U.S.A.
Penguin Group (Canada), 90 Eglinton Avenue East, Suite 700, Toronto, Ontario, Canada M4P 2Y3
(a division of Pearson Penguin Canada Inc.)
Penguin Books Ltd, 80 Strand, London WC2R 0RL, England
Penguin Ireland, 25 St Stephen's Green, Dublin 2, Ireland (a division of Penguin Books Ltd)
Penguin Group (Australia), 250 Camberwell Road, Camberwell, Victoria 3124, Australia
(a division of Pearson Australia Group Pty Ltd)
Penguin Books India Pvt Ltd, 11 Community Centre, Panchsheel Park, New Delhi - 110 017, India
Penguin Group (NZ), 67 Apollo Drive, Rosedale, North Shore 0632, New Zealand
(a division of Pearson New Zealand Ltd.)
Penguin Books (South Africa) (Pty) Ltd, 24 Sturdee Avenue,
Rosebank, Johannesburg 2196, South Africa

Registered Offices: Penguin Books Ltd, 80 Strand, London WC2R 0RL, England

First published in the United States of America by Viking, a member of Penguin Group (USA) Inc., 2009
Published by Speak, an imprint of Penguin Group (USA) Inc., 2010

3 5 7 9 10 8 6 4 2

THE LIBRARY OF CONGRESS HAS CATALOGED THE VIKING EDITION AS FOLLOWS:
Volponi, Paul.
Response / by Paul Volponi.
p. cm.
Summary: When an African American high school student is beaten with a baseball bat
in a white neighborhood, three boys are charged with a hate crime.
ISBN: 978-0-670-06283-6 (hc)
[1. Hate crimes—Fiction. 2. Prejudices—Fiction. 3. Race relations—Fiction.
4. African Americans—Fiction.] I. Title.
PZ7.V8877Re 2009 [Fic]—dc22 2008023264

Speak ISBN 978-0-14-241603-7

Printed in the United States of America

Set in ITC Century
Book design by Nancy Brennan

This text is dedicated to those moments
of insight during which we struggle so hard to break
the surface of our common pool of ignorance.

Special thanks to Joy Peskin, Regina Hayes,
Rosemary Stimola, April Volponi, and Jim Cocoros.

GOD GAVE NOAH THE RAINBOW SIGN
NO MORE WATER, THE FIRE NEXT TIME

—*Anonymous, Spiritual*

response

MY WHOLE LIFE, I'VE NEVER BEEN BRAVE. I've never stared anything down that didn't whip my ass first. That's the way it is with me, always thinking what I should have done after the time to do it is over.

That's how it was that hot August night, when those three white kids piled out of that black Land Rover screaming, "Nigger-thieves, go back to the jungle!" I was running scared before I ever saw the metal baseball bat one of them was swinging.

Deep down, I knew they were part right. I was a damn thief. I'd crossed Decatur Avenue into Hillsboro with Bonds and Asa, looking for a Lexus to heist. But I was no "nigger," not the way they meant it, even if that's what me and my friends called each other all the time.

I tripped on the cracked sidewalk, banging my chin on the concrete and scraping my palms raw. Bonds and Asa jetted down the block like their asses were lit on fire. But before I could get back up, those racist bastards were right on top of me.

I recognized the fat kid from around school—before he'd dropped out. I never knew his name. He cocked the bat in both hands, and I nearly shit myself.

The skinny dude was kicking at me when I heard the air whistle next to my left ear. *CRACK!* The fat kid had slammed me in the side of the head with that bat, and a lightning bolt of pain shot through me.

I could feel the warm blood on my face. It tasted bitter as it dripped into my mouth. For a few seconds I was seeing double, and there were six of them instead of three.

"You wanna steal from white people, huh?" screamed the tall kid with the goatee, trying to take the sneakers off my feet. "See how *you* like it!"

My legs started pedaling on instinct, like I was on a ten-speed, fighting him off.

"Give 'em over!" barked the fat kid through his clenched teeth, cocking the bat again.

I brought my arms up to protect my skull. That's when the fight in my legs quit, and they stole the sneakers. Then the tall kid dug his nails into my ear, ripping out the diamond stud. I tried to slam my fist down on his foot. But I missed, and punched the pavement instead.

They howled over that and got back into their Land Rover, giving each other high fives like they'd just won some big ball game.

My head was pounding so bad it hurt to think, but I

reached into my pocket for my cell and called Bonds.

"I need help bad," I said. "I got beat with a bat."

Then Bonds must have called 911, because a minute later I heard sirens twisting through the streets, till the cops and EMS arrived.

The next time I saw that aluminum bat, detectives were asking me to ID it in the hospital. I was lying in the intensive-care unit with tubes coming out of my arms.

Dad, Mom, and Grandma were there, too.

The bat was sealed up inside a plastic bag.

Mom shrieked at the sight of it, squeezing my hand so tight she almost cut off my pulse.

"Lord, no!" she cried. "They didn't use that on my baby!"

The meat part of the bat was stained with my blood, and some of my hair was stuck on that spot.

It was like somebody had pulled a nightmare out of my brain, holding it up in the light for me to look at.

I reached out to touch it, just to feel how solid it really was. Only the detective wouldn't let me.

"Rules of evidence," he said.

My eyes moved slowly up its black handle, with every part of me shaking. Then I saw the logo across the red aluminum barrel—the gold letters that spelled out R-E-S-P-O-N-S-E.

Chapter **ONE**

THAT AFTERNOON, ASA HAD PITCHED US HIS plan on the bench outside the Chinese take-out joint. He'd seen his uncle hot-wire his aunt's car after she lost the keys, and said it was *too* easy.

"I only needed to see it one time, Noah," he told me, between forkfuls of pork fried rice. "We can get six G's from the dude down at the chop shop for a Lex, any model. All we got to do is snatch one, deliver it, and walk away rich."

"A Lex is worth tons more than that," Bonds said.

"Yeah, but we'd only be on the hook from the time we snatched it till we dropped it off," argued Asa. "That could be just five or six minutes' work."

I was beat tired of hearing my baby's moms bitch over the fifty bucks I gave her every week from my part-time job at Mickey D's. That was more money than I took for myself, but my baby daughter was worth it.

I was going to be a "super senior" at Carver High School that September. I fell into that fifth-year hole last semester when Deshawna gave birth, and it got impossible to keep my mind on studying with everything I had to do for the baby.

But if I buckled down and passed the couple of classes I had left, I could graduate by the end of January. And I wanted to get into a city college bad, and maybe study to be an engineer like I always wanted, especially since I'd seen how it was to slave for minimum wage.

This car gig was going to be the easy way, quicker than graduating for now. It was going to shut up Deshawna about money and get me more respect with her dad. Then my own family wouldn't have to spend a dime on my daughter neither, and I could finally stop my father from saying, "Of course Noah needs help. He's just a kid supporting a kid."

Hearing Dad's voice in my head helped push me in that direction.

"You know what? Count me in. It ain't hurtin' nobody. People's insurance companies will cover it," I said, wiping the grease from an egg roll off my fingers and putting a fist out in front of me. "Besides, I'm tired of just spinnin' my wheels. I gotta make some real moves with my life."

Then Asa and Bonds stuck out their fists, too, and we connected on a three-way pound.

"But listen, anybody with a whip that fly in *this* hood's

got juice. They're either a cop or corrections officer, or runnin' game on the street," said Bonds. "We don't need those headaches. Let's slip into Hillsboro and rip off some senior citizen–white folks. The kind that's so old, it might be two days 'fore they figure out their ride's gone."

We'd been up there plenty of times before to go to the big multiplex and the mall. And Hillsboro had the best pizza parlors anywhere, because it was mostly Italian. But we knew those Guido kids didn't want us hanging around their neighborhood. Most people who lived there, Italian or anything else, looked at us like being black was something dirty and we weren't as good as them.

It didn't matter that Carver High was on the border-line between East Franklin, where *we* live, and Hillsboro. Lots of white kids who went to school with us thought the same racist way, only on the down low, out of fear of catching a black foot in their behind. I'd even heard dudes from the *other* high school in Hillsboro, Armstrong High, rank on white kids at Carver, calling them "zookeepers" for having to sit next to us in class.

"And if we're gonna snatch somebody's ride," Asa said with a smile, "it'll be sweeter doin' it there."

"Maybe we can dress up in monkey suits and say we're valet parking. They'll just hand us the damn keys," cracked Bonds.

"We just gotta watch our backs. That's all," I warned them. "'Cause the ones that really hate us are all together on it."

After that, we worked out all the little details. Then we went our separate ways home and waited for it to get dark, so we could turn our talk into action.

That night, it was steaming outside. Everybody in the city must have had their electricity on, because all the lights in our apartment were dim and the air coming out of the AC was barely cool.

Half the people in our apartment building were on the front stoop trying to catch a breeze. Dad was playing dominoes at a fold-up table, with his subway conductor's shirt wide open. He was holding seven white tiles at one time, stretched across the fingers of his two huge hands.

Mom and Grandma were talking to a bunch of neighbor women, and I could hear Grandma's strong voice over them all.

"That's not how young folks did it in my day," she said. "They acted proper and had more pride in themselves."

I'd already snuck a screwdriver out of my father's tool chest, hiding it in the back pocket of my pants. When it hit 8:45, I started down the street.

"Where you off to, Noah?" Dad called after me, slamming down a domino.

Before I could answer, Mom yelled, "He'd better be checking up on that daughter of his!"

"Right now I'm doin' it!" I hollered back, pointing to my cell as I kept on walking.

"Oh, it's you, playa," Deshawna answered, giving me the cold shoulder before she put the phone up to my daughter's ear.

"Destiny Love, this is your daddy," I said sweet. "Who's the best girl in the whole wide world? Tell me, who?"

I could hear her making noise at the sound of my voice, slapping at the phone. And right then, I wished for anything that she was cradled warm inside my arms.

Deshawna got back on and I ran her a script about the big payday I had coming.

"My boy's uncle owns a car dealership," I said. "We're gonna do some construction work on the lot for him at night—sharpen up on my building skills. That's where I'm headed now. If it goes smooth, I'll be able to triple the money I been giving you and treat you to Red Lobster for your b-day, too, boo."

"I know lately you been tryin' extra hard to do your share, Noah," she said, melting down. "I see it. Even my dad's off your case some. I really do love you."

"I feel you," I answered.

I met up with Asa and Bonds at nine o'clock sharp. They were strapped down with the other tools we needed—

wire cutters, flashlight, and a Slim Jim. Then we crossed Decatur Avenue into Hillsboro and kept our heads on a swivel.

After about a half hour, we spotted a Lex on a dark side street, parked in the driveway of a private house. We walked around the block twice just to check things out. Then we crouched down low by the gate, waiting for the courage to move.

Bonds took the Slim Jim out from under his shirt, whispering, "I'm ready to do my thing."

But as soon as Bonds started fishing for the latch to open the driver's door, there was a noise from across the street and we just froze up solid, like stone statues.

An old lady dragged her trash can all the way to the curb, with a little yappy dog barking its head off behind her—*Yappp! Yappp! Yappp!*

Finally, they disappeared inside a house, and Bonds got back to business.

I heard the latch on the car door spring open.

That's when a light on the second floor of that crib, over the driveway where we were, came on. I'm not sure who, but one us screamed soft, *"Go! Go!"*

We shot out of that yard quick, and our feet didn't stop moving till we were two blocks down and an avenue over.

"Niggas can't get jumpy over every little shit," complained Asa, breathing hard. "There's gonna be some risk."

"Noah, wasn't this boy the first one hauling ass?" Bonds asked between breaths, annoyed as anything.

But the bottom of my kicks had burned rubber, too, and I wasn't about to front over having nerves of steel.

"We *all* looked like kindergarten crooks," I said flat-out.

Mario's Pizza came up on the other side of the street, so we cooled our jets and went inside for a slice. There was a map of Italy, looking like a boot, painted up on the wall. A rotating floor fan was blowing hard, and a little red-white-and-green flag taped to the cash register flapped in that breeze.

Two Guido kids with slicked-back hair and gold chains were sitting at a side table, giving us the evil eye. And the chain on the one who had a goatee was thick enough to get us nearly as much cheddar as a hot car.

But I'd have rather made him eat it, instead, for giving us that look.

We each ordered a slice and a soda, and the dude behind the counter smirked. "Is that order to go?"

"Nah, too much heat out there," Asa answered with some attitude.

The goateed kid yelled out to that dude, "Hey, Sal! Make me an order of eggplant Parmesan—moolie style!"

That's what Italian assholes called us, "moolies."

I heard that in their tongue, *moolinyan* meant egg-plant. That was their code word for *nigger*, because we were black like eggplants.

Asa stared that kid down fierce, drawing the bottom half of a circle under his neck with a finger to show that Guido's gold chain could have been ours if we wanted it. But we finished our food and got out of there without any trouble.

Our stomachs were heavy by then, so we gave up on the idea of boosting a Lex that night.

There wasn't a dark cloud I could see anywhere, but streaks of heat lightning kept crackling across the sky as we headed back towards East Franklin. We even walked the long way around, steering clear of Columbus Park— the place almost everybody called "Spaghetti Park," the Guidos' main turf.

We were just three blocks from Decatur Ave. when those two dudes from the pizza parlor and that fat kid swinging the baseball bat jumped out of the Land Rover screaming, "Niggers!"

CHARLIE SCAT

Nobody's snatching Joey's chain. Nobody. Not here. Not while I'm still breathing. My crew knows who to call when shit jumps off. I couldn't get dressed and out of my front door fast enough. I hate these nigger-thieves. Hate them. They know where they belong—East Franklin. Not by us. First, they piss all over their own neighborhood till it's nothing but stink. Now they want to do they same here? Fuck that.

"That them? There? I'll pull over! Everybody out, quick!"

Look at 'em run. That's it. Be scared.

Shit. That one bagged himself.

Stay right there. Stay down, you mother.

"Leave 'em, Tommy! Move outta the way!"

Taste bat.

I'll split his damn skull like a coconut.

"Yeah! Take his shoes, Joey! Take those shits!"

Go ahead, do something. Try it. I'll give you another taste of this.

"Rip his earring out! Rip it!"

He probably stuck up somebody's grandmother to buy that bling crap.

"Don't let his blood touch you! Don't touch it, you'll catch somethin'!"

No fight in him. Nothing. Another coward.

Only with half their projects behind 'em they act tough.

I'm supposed to sit in school with them. No way.

That's another thing they fucked up, with their music and gangs.

They think they can get our girls, too.

Kiss my fat ass now. Kiss it, mother.

I'm never getting in line behind you. Never. I'm far back enough.

Remember who am I.

I told you. I told you who I was.

"Gimme five! Yeah! Gimme some skin, boys!"

I'm somebody with this bat.

I told you. See.

Chapter **TWO**

I REMEMBERED BONDS AND ASA BEING there with the cops and EMS. I couldn't get up off the concrete, or even move without mad pains shooting through my entire body. My head was killing me, and it hurt to keep my eyes open. So I tried to hold them shut.

"Who beat you, son? What did they look like? Why do you think they jumped you?" the cops were asking.

More than anything, I wanted to nail the fat fuck swinging that bat, and see those bastards do the perp-walk in cuffs. But I'd been through shit with police before and arrested twice—once for a stupid fight and another time for beating the fare on a city bus. And my whole family was just starting to trust me again.

I knew some of those white cops in Hillsboro weren't any better than the kids who'd beat me. They'd kick your ass, too. Only the cops had badges to make it *legal*, and could turn anything you said against them into an automatic lie.

"Bat! Bat!" I kept yelling. "Hurts too much to think!"

I was scared to death the cops would arrest us for trying to boost that car. I was the one who'd fucked up and tripped, and maybe that was going to land the three of us in central booking.

Then a cop asked, "You want to explain about this screwdriver in your pocket?"

After that, I wouldn't say another word, and kept my mouth and eyes shut. Bonds and Asa clammed up tight, too. I remember EMS lifting me into the ambulance on a stretcher, and the sound of that siren pounded inside my skull all the way to the hospital.

That's when it hit me for real. The fat kid could have killed me with that damn bat. I'd have never held Destiny Love in my arms again or been there the first time she said "Daddy" for real. He almost stole everything from me, just because my skin was a different color than his.

Bonds told me later how some black cop pulled him and Asa off to the side.

"You going to let these white punks draw a line with a bat, sayin' where you can't be? Let them shit all over you like that?" the black cop railed on them. "And that's your *friend*—the young brother on the stretcher? Why don't you boys just crawl home from here if you ain't got the bellies to stand up for him or yourselves?"

Maybe it was seeing me leave with my skull split open, or maybe it was that speech, but Bonds and Asa agreed to ride in the back of a squad car, searching for those bastards who busted me up. They spotted that black Land Rover parked on the same block as Mario's Pizza. But as soon as the cops pulled up behind it, those three white dudes got out cool as ice, pointing at Asa and Bonds in the police car.

"That's them, officers!" the fat kid shouted, clapping his hands. "The ones that tried to rob my friends! Lock 'em up!"

Then Asa said half of the 14th Precinct showed up. He said one of the white cops must have tipped them dudes off about the screwdriver, because that's what they started saying—that we tried to rob them for a gold chain using a screwdriver like a knife.

But not every cop had their backs. And after a search, other officers found the bat and my sneakers inside the Land Rover, and my diamond stud in the tall kid's pocket.

Bonds and Asa had to come clean to explain about that screwdriver, and told the cops how we went into Hillsboro to heist a car. To prove it, they took the cops back to the spot where they'd ditched the Slim Jim, wire cutters, and flashlight—inside some Dumpster on the street, after Bonds had called 911.

Finally, the three of those racist bastards got arrested. That was probably about the same time the doctors were bringing me into surgery for my skull. The same time

Dad, Mom, and Grandma were praying to God with every breath they took that I'd be all right. The same time that Destiny Love was sound asleep in her crib at Deshawna's house.

The cops let Bonds and Asa skate that night, but everything was about to blow up huge. The next day, the mayor and police commissioner came to Hillsboro and a special squad of detectives got called in to investigate, to see if what happened was just a regular robbery and beat-down by those dudes, or something much bigger—a hate crime.

EMS brought me to the closest hospital—St. Luke's in Hillsboro. When I woke up from my operation the next morning, the first thing I saw was the white ceiling of that room. Then my eyes started to focus, and I saw Mom's face lean in. For a second, I dreamed I was at home and had overslept for school. So I tried to jerk myself up fast. That's when the pain in my head hit hard.

"Ooow!" I cried out as that nightmare with the bat ripped through my brain in fast-forward.

"Thank you, Jesus!" boomed Grandma's voice. "Thank *you*!"

Mom broke down bawling on my chest, and Dad put his arms around us both.

"Noah, whatever your mother and me done wrong in

our lives couldn't have been so bad," my father said, with his face looking older and more tired than I'd ever seen it. "'Cause when you just opened your eyes, God answered all our prayers."

The surgeon who'd operated on me was from India, and his skin was nearly as dark as mine.

"The fracture was serious enough that I couldn't take a conservative approach and let it heal on its own. I put some fragments of loose skull back into place and secured them with a small titanium plate and screws," he told us. "We'll keep monitoring Noah for any signs of infection or intracranial hemorrhaging—bleeding on the brain. But other than some potential headaches and bruising around the eyes, which I see has begun already, he should be all right to go home in about a week or so."

Mom looked like she was about to drown that doctor in hugs. But Dad stepped to him first and shook his hand. So that's what Mom and Grandma did, too, clasping both of their hands around his.

I wanted to argue about having to stay in the hospital so long, but what came out instead was, "Thanks for what you did, Doc."

Then he reached down and touched me on the left shoulder, I guess before I messed up any of the tubes in my arms, trying to reach across to shake his hand.

There were three nurses at the station outside my

door—one was black and the other two were white. And any time one of those whites nurses came at me with a needle to take blood, every muscle in my body would pull tight till the veins in my arms popped out on their own.

That night, Mom apologized to those two white nurses after they heard her call the bastards who'd beat me "no good crackers" and "white trash."

"Nobody needs to say they're sorry for the truth!" Grandma exploded after those nurses left the room.

"I feel they're the ones caring for my boy," Mom argued back. "So I don't want to insult them."

"They've heard it before—seen it, too," said Dad. "Noah ain't the first one to catch a beating on those streets."

"Pray he's the last," said Grandma. "Pray *Noah's* the last!"

Then my father said, "I remember how that man—Sheffield—they killed, got brought to this same hospital before he died."

That happened almost twenty years ago. I wasn't even born yet. But people around my way still talked about it plenty, and I knew every word of that story by heart.

These four black dudes from Centreville, just one neighborhood over from East Franklin, had their car break down on the highway at the far edge of Hillsboro. Back then, everybody didn't have cell phones like now, so they started walking. Only they picked the wrong direction to go in. Those brothers wound up over by Spaghetti Park. It was on a weekend night in the summer, and the park was really popping. Just for showing up there, a pack of white thugs chased them down Decatur. One of the black dudes, Michael Sheffield, got run off into traffic and was clipped and killed by a car. Something like fifty people saw it, but nobody from Hillsboro would be a witness at the trial. That's why just three thugs out of that whole mob got convicted.

The only reason Sheffield was dead was because he was black. So it got called a "hate crime" and made headlines all over the country. People in Hillsboro were still pissed over that kind of attention, because now whenever somebody said the name "Hillsboro," all anybody thought about was a place full of racist, murdering fucks.

"There's a street named after him in Centreville—Sheffield Street," I said, struggling to sit up in my bed. "I was even standing on it one time."

"They shoulda renamed Decatur Avenue for him," Dad said. "Then everybody around here who shut their eyes to that killing would have had to see that sign every damn day."

Deshawna's dad wouldn't let her go into Hillsboro alone after dark. So they both came to visit me that first night, bringing along my six-month-old baby daughter. Destiny Love didn't stop crying from the second she got into that hospital room. My head was pounding from the noise, but that didn't matter. I wanted her right there in my arms.

Nobody in my family had pressed me yet on what I was doing in Hillsboro.

Then Deshawna asked, "Noah, did they jump you before you got to the car lot to do that construction job, or after?"

I swallowed hard and answered over my daughter's wailing, "There was no construction job. We went there for the wrong reason—to boost a car."

I could see the shame creep into my father's and Grandma's faces, especially in front of Deshawna's dad.

And by then the purple bruising around my eyes looked like a thief's mask, like the Hamburglar character at Mickey D's wore.

"But you didn't take nobody's car, right?" Mom asked, defiant. "Then why did they beat you with that bat? It was because you're black. That's why! And nobody's gonna twist it around!"

After the shame left my father's face, he began to stare darts at me.

I wanted to hide. But there was nowhere to go, except under the sheets.

The next morning, the doctor said it was all right for the detectives to ask me questions. They showed me a bunch of mug shots, too, and I picked out all three of those kids who'd beat me.

"That's the one swinging the bat," I said, stamping my finger down into the middle of the fat kid's face. "He was at Carver High with me for a hot minute."

"That's Charles Scaturro—known on the streets as Charlie Scat," said the black detective. "He's got a history of assaults on nonwhites."

The kid with the goatee was named Joseph Spenelli.

"Scaturro and Spenelli are being held without bail. The third suspect you identified, Thomas Rao, is also in custody. *He's* cooperating with the investigation," added his white partner.

"Good. Let them turn on each other now," Grandma said.

"But this Rao won't get a free pass for talking?" Dad asked, concerned.

"Nobody will," the white detective answered like he meant it. "We don't play those kind of games."

"We've determined that none of the suspects knew you were there to steal a car before the beating. So they weren't acting as vigilantes, trying to take the law into their own hands," said his partner. "And because racial epithets were used during the attack, this is going to be prosecuted as a hate crime."

Mom stood there applauding over that.

"Amen," she said between claps. "Amen."

But those words—"hate crime"—echoed in my ears.

I went to sleep that night with the worst headache I'd ever had.

And the next morning, I woke up the same way.

CHARLES SCATURRO INTERVIEW

The two detectives and Charlie Scat are seated in a small interrogation room (one wall is a mirrored panel) at the police precinct, with just a thin wooden table and a tape recorder between them.

WHITE DETECTIVE: Tell us again, Charlie.

CHARLIE SCAT: I was walkin' with my boys and—

BLACK DETECTIVE: Where were you headed?

CHARLIE SCAT: Over by Spaghetti, just to chill. Then these three guys we don't know—

WHITE DETECTIVE: Three *black* guys?

CHARLIE SCAT: Yeah. You know, African Americans.

BLACK DETECTIVE: It was pretty dark out. Did you see their faces or just their smiles?

CHARLIE SCAT: Look. It's not like that. I swear.

WHITE DETECTIVE: Go on, Charlie.

CHARLIE SCAT: So these guys see Joey's gold chain—it's a real nice one, thick. I even told him, "Joey, you gotta be careful the places you wear that." I mean, but this is *our* (*Taps his chest.*) neighborhood for Christ's sake. Then one of them says loud, "Look at the white nigger—thinks he can hold down that chain!" They pulled a screwdriver on us. But we just fought 'em off, and they ran. Then we got into my car and tried to find them.

BLACK DETECTIVE: You didn't call 911?

CHARLIE SCAT: Honestly, we were so pissed, we weren't thinkin' straight.

WHITE DETECTIVE: And the bat? Where'd that come from?

CHARLIE SCAT: That's always in the car. For protection. You need it these days. Sometimes I drive my mother to get her hair done just on the other side of Decatur.

BLACK DETECTIVE: So you found them and fractured Noah Jackson's skull with that bat?

CHARLIE SCAT: No. No. He musta did that when he tripped. He probably hit his head on the sidewalk or something.

WHITE DETECTIVE: How'd he lose his sneakers and earring?

CHARLIE SCAT: I think they just came off while we was tryin' to hold him down. Then we kept them to give to the cops, while we chased those other two.

BLACK DETECTIVE: Did you use any epithets?

CHARLIE SCAT: Any what?

WHITE DETECTIVE: Did you call them names?

CHARLIE SCAT: Just "nigger." There's nothing wrong with that. That's what they call each other all the time. You ever hear their music? It's all "nigger" this, and "nigger" that.

BLACK DETECTIVE: So how come you don't call me a nigger, Charlie?

CHARLIE SCAT: You know. (*Fights back a grin.*) 'Cause I want to get outta here and go home.

Chapter **THREE**

THAT SATURDAY, WHILE I WAS STILL IN THE
hospital, there was a big march through Hillsboro. Black
leaders showed up from all over the city, and there were
even two busloads of brothers from out of town. The
TV news said there were over six hundred protesters,
with more than a hundred white folks mixed in. They
started out on Decatur Avenue where Michael Sheffield
died. Then they marched past the spot where I got beat
down, and all the way to Spaghetti Park.

Dad and Mom were at the head of the line, walking hand in hand with those leaders. People had done
the same thing when Sheffield got killed. Thousands of
marchers showed up back then. Only Michael Sheffield
wasn't there to steal a car, and I knew there wouldn't be
any petition to name a street after me.

"The last time we were here, nearly two decades ago,
they lined up to throw watermelon rinds at us. Now some
of the store owners are offering us bottled water to drink

as we march," a gray-haired black city councilman told the TV reporter. "I guess that's progress for *this* community. But that hasn't solved the tensions and intolerable crime of racial violence."

I watched the screen with Grandma. We were both hyped to see that many black people rolling through Hillsboro, and with a police escort, too. The news showed how Spaghetti Park was packed with white people protesting right back. Somebody even took a bedsheet and painted the words BATS AND CAR THIEVES inside a big circle with a strike mark through it.

"We don't want to be known for this kind of thing anymore," said a lady being interviewed. "Good people live here. Can't we be left alone in our own neighborhoods? We just want this to all go away."

The white nurse who was taking my temperature stopped cold while that lady was talking. Her eyes were glued to the TV screen and she was nodding her head, when Grandma said in a sharp tone, "That woman's wrong. You can't ignore a cancer. But she don't know nothing about healing like *you* do."

"Why, th-ank you," the nurse answered through half a stutter.

All together, I stayed at St. Luke's for nine days. My last two days there, I was feeling almost back to normal and itching to get out, with a rep from Dad's insurance company pushing for me to leave, too. When the doctors finally said I could go home, they made me ride downstairs in a wheelchair, because that was their insurance rule. But as soon as those sliding-glass doors opened, and I took my first hit of outside air without that sterilized hospital smell to it, I jumped up to my feet fast.

There were a few reporters waiting outside the hospital, and one asked how I felt about the kids who beat me. That's when Mom wrapped both her arms around me, and I didn't fight her on it.

"I don't feel anything for them, like they didn't feel anything for me," I answered.

"Do you hate them, Noah?" another one asked.

"I don't have love for nobody like that," I said, with my hand balling up into a fist at my side.

"How about the one with the bat, Charles Scaturro? Is there something you'd like to say to him?"

"How do you feel about white people, Noah? Can you trust them?"

The questions started flying.

"I just, just—" I said, shaking my head, without any more words coming.

There were only curses in my brain, and I knew enough not to say them.

Then my father told those reporters it was time for us to go home, and they backed off.

The first cab driver in line outside the hospital was white.

"We're going to East Franklin—Twelfth and Dupont," Dad told him.

But the driver said, smug, "I don't go over by there. That's off my assigned route."

It took a second for what he'd said to sink in.

Then Mom roared, "Take down his damn license number!"

"You see this?" my father called to the reporters. "What happened to my son—it doesn't change *shit*!"

Asa and Bonds had been keeping a low profile and hadn't come to see me in the hospital even once. I didn't hold it against them, though. I'd have been covering my ass, too, if I could, hoping the cops wouldn't find any charges against me. But the second day I was home, Bonds called me on my cell to say they were both coming over and Mom overheard me talking.

"Tell your criminal-minded friends they're not welcome inside this apartment," Mom said, cold. "And from now on, as long as you're livin' under this roof, Noah, I want to know where you are, twenty-four/seven."

So I watched out the window and went downstairs to meet them on the stoop as they turned the corner. Every building on the block was an exact Xerox copy of mine—a four-story, eight-family apartment house filled with black families.

Only the colors on the *outside* of them were different.

Even as a little kid digging in a flower box with a toy steam shovel, I remember wanting to plow those houses under and rebuild each one again to be special.

Halfway down the block there were a bunch of kids in bathing suits making noise, running through the spray of a fire hydrant with a sprinkler cap on it. Asa and Bonds must have ducked through, too, because I could see their wet footprints behind them, fading into the hot pavement.

"Daaaamn," said Asa, seeing the patch of stitches in my head. "That's no joke when they operate on somebody's skull."

"How you been holding up, dog?" Bonds asked as I gave them both a pound, before pulling them in close for a hug. "You know those crackers can't break a strong black man."

"I'm all right. I guess," I answered.

That's when somebody's grandmother, from a stoop across the street, called out, "Noah, God bless you," and blew me a kiss.

"You a celebrity, Noah." Asa grinned. "Everybody's talking 'bout how you stand for something now—almost like Rosa Parks."

"Nah, I'm just history in my own crib," I said, looking up at Mom peeping us through the curtains of our third-floor window. "I'm the most famous dude under house arrest in East Franklin."

"I know it," moaned Bonds. "My mom's got the shackles out, too—*Where ya goin'? Whataya doin'? Who ya be with?*—meanwhile I'm thinking, my boy almost got killed. It's time for war."

"Nobody can touch them punks," Asa said. "You *know* they're in protective custody, each with a cell to himself. Cops can't put those dudes in population. Niggas will tear their asses up."

That was the first time I'd heard that word *nigger* since Scat screamed it at me. And suddenly, I didn't like it any better coming easy from Asa's mouth.

"One of them's out," said Bonds. "It was on the radio before."

I felt the blood rushing to my brain, and all I could see was red.

"Which?" I asked.

"One whose father's a detective, ratting out the other two," answered Bonds. "The kid who kicked you. That Ra-O."

"Oooh! Somebody needs to clap that cracker," said Asa, throwing a right cross and stamping his foot on the steps.

"So his father's got a badge," I said, hawking a wad of spit onto the street and wishing I'd clammed it into the face of that white detective in the hospital who'd promised "nobody" would get a free pass.

"Sherlock Holmes to the bone. Everybody knows they take care of their own kind," Bonds said. "But we didn't come here to amp you up. We wanted to set things straight."

"See-we-didn't-know-you-tripped," Asa said, beating a rhythm on his palm with the back of his other hand. "I was, like, fifty feet out in front of Bonds. I figured you was behind him."

"I seen that bat and I was too busy bookin'," said Bonds, more serious than I'd ever heard him. "I thought I was bringing up the rear and you was way out in front, Noah. You didn't call out or nothin'. And if you did, I didn't hear it."

"We'd have never left you one on three against them animals," said Asa, pounding his chest with a fist. "We was on a mission together. That's blood, right there."

At first I'd felt like a fuckup for falling and causing everything that night, and part of me still did.

"People around here been busting on us for not having your back," Bonds said, looking me in the eye. "I don't need that kind of rep, 'specially when school starts up."

"I'm good with it," I said, my stomach going tight into

knots over that Rao getting turned loose. "That's just the way it went down."

"Yo, when the cops drove us around Hillsboro, we seen your old Air Jordans," said Asa. "They're still hanging right where you left them, almost four years now, over that phone wire in the Crackers' Hall of Fame."

As freshman, for half a season, the three of us played JV football together for Carver, till our grades came out and we flunked off the team. One Saturday morning, the school took us by bus to play at the athletic field that connects up to Spaghetti Park. Our squad was mixed, and the Armstrong High team was all white. Their guys were bragging about the "Hall of Fame." It was just a phone wire that ran across the street next to the field with maybe forty pairs of old cleats hanging on it.

"After we stomp some black ass, we'll vote our best player to hang his shoes up there," one of them cackled.

The game was nasty, with lots of kicks and punches from both squads at the bottom of every pileup. Then, with the score tied in the fourth quarter, the rain started coming down in buckets and wouldn't stop. You could hardly see in front of your face, and after five minutes that field was nothing but a muddy pit.

On the next-to-last play of the game, their quarterback threw a pass that got tipped in the air. By dumb luck it came down right into my hands. I started running for the end zone as fast as I could, with half their dudes hot on my tail. I sank deeper into the mud with every step, and it was like running in quicksand. My thighs and lungs were burning. I didn't even have on football cleats. I was wearing Jordans. But I made it past what was left of that white-chalk goal line before one of *them* shoved me face-first into the mud.

My teammates were jumping on top of me, celebrating, even the white ones. And after we won, Armstrong's players used the rain as an excuse not to shake our hands.

We changed our clothes back on the bus, and our guys were calling it "Noah's Ark."

Then Asa, Bonds, and me went back outside on the low. The street was empty with all that rain pounding down, and I tossed those muddy sneakers over the phone wire on my first try.

NEW ATTACK OPENS OLD WOUNDS
From *The Morning Star Herald*

On a stifling summer afternoon, Columbus Park offers barely an inch of shade. Its 14-foot-high chain-link fence encloses a handball wall, swings, monkey bars, sprinklers, and benches spread out over half a city block of asphalt. For almost two decades, this ordinary-looking playground in the nearly all-white section of Hillsboro has been called a den of hatred and intolerance by surrounding black communities. On the street it is known as Spaghetti Park, due to the large number of Italian American teens who hang out there. The park was the igniting point of the 1990 killing of African American Michael Sheffield, who was struck down by a car as he fled from an angry mob of white teenagers.

"It's safe here. Everybody knows everybody else," said Diana DeBlassi, a 16-year-old sophomore at nearby Armstrong High School. "My parents let me stay here with my friends at night because they know I'll be all right."

On August 9, just six blocks from Columbus Park, three African American teens from East Franklin were chased, and 17-year-old Noah Jackson was beaten in the head with an aluminum baseball bat. And once again, Hillsboro is in the headlines as the site of an alleged hate crime.

"It wasn't anything racial," said a distraught Delores Scaturro, the mother of bat-wielding suspect, Charles Scaturro, 18. "They're trying to make my son pay for what happened here twenty years ago. The mayor and DA are playing politics with his life to score points with the blacks in the next election."

Charles Scaturro, who is being held without bail, is currently on probation for firing a paint gun at a Pakistani couple on the streets of Hillsboro. A high-school dropout who has a $40,000 Land Rover registered in his name, Scaturro is unemployed.

Also charged in the hate-crime assault on Jackson is Joseph Spenelli, 18, who allegedly beat and robbed the teen of his sneakers and diamond-stud earring. Spenelli is also being held without bail. As of yet, no charges have been filed against a third suspected attacker, Thomas Rao, 17, whose father, Anthony Rao, is a city detective. Thomas Rao is cooperating with authorities.

"That's what the (expletive) police do in this neighborhood now. They set traps for young people. Then they try to turn them against each other to survive," said Delores Scaturro.

After successful surgery on his fractured skull, Noah Jackson, a senior at Carver High School, which Charles Scaturro also once attended, is now recuperating at home.

Jackson, who has a pair of juvenile arrests on his record, admittedly was in Hillsboro with his companions to steal a car.

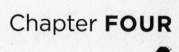

Chapter **FOUR**

I'D MISSED A LITTLE MORE THAN TWO WEEKS
of work at Mickey D's. Then I found out from Deshawna
that my father had given her a C-note to help take care
of Destiny Love while I was in the hospital. He never said
anything to me about it. And that was the first time he
hadn't flattened me with his mouth over helping out with
money.

"I wasn't the one who had any of that *bedroom fun*,
but I'm the one who's got to pay," Dad would say. "I'd have
been happier to give you the money for condoms, son. It
would have been cheaper."

But mad as my father would get, it all melted away any
time he bounced Destiny Love on his lap.

Deshawna went to Carver High, too. Only she'd
dropped out of regular classes just before she had our
baby, and was taking a GED class in the school's base-
ment, along with Asa. We weren't planning on getting
married or anything. At least I wasn't.

I still wasn't 100 percent sold that I was in love with

her, and other shorties were always catching my eye. But I knew for certain I was in love with my daughter, and that *she'd* always be a part of my life, no matter what.

I'd been dating Deshawna for six months when she got pregnant.

She never had a thought that she wouldn't keep the baby. So there was nothing I could really say on the subject.

Deshawna was scared to death to tell her dad and wanted me to be there with her.

"I'll break the news," I said, acting confident. "I can handle it."

I even had the words laid out in my head from practicing them over and over—*It's not something Deshawna and me were planning, but it happened. She's pregnant, and I'm the baby's father. So I'm going to do what's right—what a man's gotta do.*

But when I looked Deshawna's dad in the eye, I turned paralyzed with fear and couldn't say a thing.

Deshawna finally burst into tears, screaming, "I'm pregnant, Daddy! I'm sorry, but I'm pregnant!"

Then she jumped into *his* arms. He was hugging her tight, grilling the shit out of me with his high beams tattooed onto mine. And I felt like less than half a man standing there alone.

We didn't even have to tell my family when we got to

my place. Deshawna had been crying all day. So when they saw her red, swollen eyes and the two of us holding hands, they figured it out straight off.

Mom and Grandma both blamed Deshawna, like she should have been ten times smarter about it than me.

"Girl, don't you know these boys only got one thing on their minds?" bristled Mom. "*You* need to have the brains that *they* don't!"

I wanted to stick up for myself, but I didn't.

"A lesson too late for the learning, child," Grandma told her, plain.

But Dad was pissed at *me*, and knocked on my head with his knuckles like it was hollow inside.

My first Friday back at Mickey D's, kids who worked there crowded around me, asking how I was. Maybe it was my imagination, but there were two white kids on the outside of that circle who looked like they couldn't care less if I'd come back a cripple. Then the manager, a white dude named Gavin Munch, barked at everybody to get back to their stations.

Munch was always a crab, acting like we were in the army, instead of serving up fast food. That's because he was almost thirty years old, and this was his *real* job.

"Can't you cover that?" said Munch, pointing at the patch of stitches in my skull. "It's the customers that are supposed to get the attention. Not the workers."

Munch had a buzz cut, and I'd even dreamed of flipping burgers off the top of his flat head. But I just held my tongue and pushed the paper hat part of my uniform over to the side.

"There you go, *boss*," I answered, pissed, walking over to the deep fryer. "All covered up. Like it never happened."

About an hour into my shift, the girl on the drive-through register got sick, and Munch hollered for me to take her place while she was in the bathroom.

People ordered over the squawk box, talking into a clown's face. Then they'd drive around to the side window where they picked up their food and paid.

My Mickey D's is off the highway exit, just outside of East Franklin and a few blocks from the start of Hillsboro—close to Carver High. So the customers are mostly mixed. But every kid I knew, white or black, called that space no-man's-land, because there was no hood you could lean on for backup if you ran into any drama there.

That whole time I was on the window, I was uptight listening to people's voices, trying to figure out who they were. I'd never stressed over anything like that before I took that beating with the bat.

Then a bunch of rowdy dudes drove up, yelling their orders over each other's. They changed around everything they wanted—twice.

"Got it right now, clowny?" one of them asked, nasty.

"You'd better or it's *free*!" snapped another one.

I knew in my bones they'd be white, and they were.

The total came to twenty-three bucks and ninety-nine cents.

They looked through every bag, like I was too stupid to get their order right.

I went to hand them the penny change and the driver cracked, "Keep it, *bro*. Buy your family something nice."

The five of them howled like a car full of hyenas, and pulled away with me holding that brown penny. I looked Abe Lincoln dead square in the face. But he just stared off to the side, like my problems weren't his. Then I slammed that penny to the ground wishing I'd spit into their food.

I got home that night around six thirty, tired as anything. But I opened the front door and saw Grandma feeding Destiny Love her bottle. That picked me right up.

Destiny Love slept over at our apartment every other weekend and this was my weekend to have her.

Deshawna was there, too. We were going out and my family was going to babysit. Then Mom called me into her bedroom and handed me a long, thin box with a blue bow. Deshawna's birthday passed while I was in the hospital, and I'd forgot all about it.

"Am I more interested in this girl than you are?" Mom whispered to me, sarcastic.

Deshawna loved the wristwatch inside, and I took her by bus to the new multiplex in Centreville. Before the flick, she caught me checking out a shorty in the next row, but I started talking fast and said, "Nobody else's watch looks as sharp as that one on you."

And she backed off, half smiling.

There were some steamy sex scenes in the movie, and the two of us started kissing. Then I let my hands take a walk where they wanted. We were both into it, but we didn't have any place to go. Since our daughter was born, we'd only had sex twice—both times at Deshawna's house, while her dad was at work.

I didn't have money for a motel or anything like that. And I wasn't about to do my baby's moms on some park bench. So I let all that heat just pass.

Later, Deshawna wanted to stop for something to eat. I was working a double shift at Mickey D's the next day, and I didn't want to see another Big Mac. But there was a Taco Bell close by and we went inside for a burrito and soda.

"I'm going to get my nails done tomorrow with my girls," she said from across the table. "Then on Sunday, Daddy's taking me shopping for new jeans."

"I got no work Sunday. I'll probably take Destiny Love to the playground and push her on the kiddie swings," I said, sipping my soda as I noticed Deshawna's eyes focusing behind me.

"Noah, look at what that girl's got on," she said, jutting her jaw towards a corner table.

There were some white girls sitting there, and one of them was wearing a T-shirt that read FREE SPENELLI!

"I feel like tearin' the shirt right off that snow bitch," growled Deshawna.

But I wouldn't let her. And I got us out of there quick before she started something, or somebody recognized me.

"What's with you, Noah?" she asked. "I know you ain't scared of those girls."

"I seen enough drama lately," I answered. "And we don't need them calling the cops on *us* now."

I took Deshawna home, and her dad watched me tight all the time I was there.

When I got back to my place, my father was sitting in his chair reading the newspaper.

"Looks like the city's gonna let the detective's son— that Rao kid—walk for testifying," said Dad, scowling.

Only it felt more like a swipe at me, like I was supposed to do something about it. So I didn't even tell him about the T-shirt, before I took the blame for that, too.

I knew part of that anger from him was about me planning to steal that car.

"It's just a big game to them," I said, heading for my room.

"But it's about *our* lives—what *we're* worth in this city that's hanging in the balance," I heard him say from behind me.

I was already feeling a ton of pressure and I didn't even think about saying something back.

There was a night-light on in my room, by Destiny Love's crib. The light was in the shape of a black angel with wings blowing a horn.

I kissed my daughter on her forehead while she was sleeping. Then I wrapped my hands around the wooden bars of her crib, watching her chest rise up and down, breathing peaceful.

It was just after midnight, and I set the clock-radio alarm on low for 6:00 A.M., to make the breakfast shift at those damn golden arches. My head hit the pillow and I was out cold. But at 3:31, Destiny Love shook me out of my sleep when she started crying for her bottle. Only that formula wasn't enough. She needed me to hold her, too. And every time I put Destiny Love back down, she screamed like the whole world was coming to an end.

I tried to leave her be. But I couldn't.

"Noah?" Mom called out. "You taking care of that?"

"Right away," I answered.

Whenever Mom got woke by Destiny Love in the middle of the night, she'd say things like, "Now if I wanted more children I'd have had them myself," or "I thought I'd get a longer break in between being a mother and a grandmother."

I had to walk the floor with Destiny Love on my shoulder for almost forty minutes, looking at the clock and trying to figure out how much more sleep I could get if I got back into bed that second.

Finally, Destiny Love fell asleep. Then I laid her down in her crib and went back to bed.

Less than two hours later, I woke up to the alarm, half dazed.

I left Destiny Love sleeping and the door to my room wide open so Mom or Grandma could hear if she needed anything.

But I'd got dressed in the dark and didn't realize I put on a regular T-shirt and not a blue uniform shirt till I'd closed our apartment door behind me and was halfway down the stairs.

CHARLIE SCAT

(Alone in his cell doing sets of push-ups, sweating)

Six feet by ten feet. Every time I pace it off, it's the same.

Cinder-block wall, cinder-block wall, cinder-block wall, and iron bars.

A metal sink and stinking toilet bowl.

For what? What did I do?

Protecting the damn neighborhood. That's all.

They had to kill that fuck twenty years ago. I'm paying for that now.

Locked down alone twenty-three hours a day, and one hour out for exercise. Like I can't make it in here, because jail's nigger country.

Bring them on. Bring them all on. I don't care.

I'll hold my weight.

Come on. Another set. I can do it.

Forty-one . . . forty-two . . . forty-threee . . . forty-fourrrr . . . forty-fiiive.

Those black bastards couldn't stay in the projects.

They couldn't keep themselves in East Fucking Franklin.

Then they get their ass whipped and go crying to the cops.

"Oh, it's a hate crime. He hates me because I'm black."

What shit! Stay where the fuck you belong!

And Tommy Rao. My friend—a rat, first class.

Like he didn't do shit that night.

"Charlie, niggers were at Mario's like they owned

the place, eyein' Joey's chain. Let's kick their asses back to the projects before more of them get ideas."

All because his father's a cop. That's why the special treatment.

Fuck his whole scab family. I hope they run every Rao out of Hillsboro.

Rat bastards, every one of them, out to save their own skin.

No honor.

Now I'm the fall guy. Well, fuck that.

So if my dead father, rest his soul, was a detective, I wouldn't be here. Right?

Blue or black, that's what you have to be in this city.

I'll stare laser beams through that punk if he ever testifies against me.

The cops are probably trying to flip Joey against me, too.

A setup. That's all it is.

My mother better mortgage the house to get that big-time lawyer. That's all I know.

Do it, Charlie. Do it. One more set. Watch those biceps pump up.

Look at those guns, big boy.

Forty-six . . . forty-seven . . . forty-eighhht . . . for-ty-niiiine . . .

Chapter **FIVE**

THE WEDNESDAY AFTER LABOR DAY, SCHOOL
started up, and there were kids from Hillsboro wearing that FREE SPENELLI! T-shirt. Not a lot of them, but
enough so I couldn't miss it. I started wondering which
other white kids thought the exact same way but didn't
have the guts to wear that shirt to school, or their parents
wouldn't let them.

Some kids from Hillsboro were just the opposite and
even told me things like, *It's wrong what happened
to you. I'm ashamed the way some people from my
neighborhood act. We don't all think like that, Noah.*

I believed them, all right. But I wasn't sure how many
of those kids would really have my back if the shit ever hit
the fan in front of them.

Maybe they'd just take the easy way out, closing their
doors and disappearing on me, knowing they'd have to
face their racist neighbors every day after that.

That's the way Carver High was. Everybody seemed

to play the lines already painted out for them. And few kids ever crossed them.

My social-studies teacher was a light-skinned black dude named Mr. Dowling. All I knew about him was that some black kids called Dowling an "Oreo cookie"—black on the outside and white on the inside—because they said he played every racial thing at Carver down the middle and never really leaned over to *our* side much.

I began to feel that way, too, when I complained to him about those T-shirts after class.

"Remember, I'm supposed to be a teacher to *all* the students here," he said. "I don't agree with those stupid shirts. But it's free speech. So you better get used to it and stay focused, Noah. Anyway, I shouldn't discourage my students from taking a political interest in anything."

But maybe Dowling went home and took a long look in the mirror. Because when three white kids showed up to class wearing those shirts the next day, Dowling changed their seats. He moved every one of them to the back row and made me sit up front.

"Just because you're exercising your constitutional rights, that doesn't mean Mr. Jackson should have to look at you all period long," he told them.

Those kids complained about it like anything, saying Dowling only did it because he was black, and that it was "reverse discrimination."

"I'll tell you what," Dowling answered. "I'll move any black students wearing that same shirt to the back row, too."

That put an end to all the arguing, right there.

I was making up eleventh- and twelfth-grade physical education, after failing them both for being unprepared—coming to class without my gym clothes ten or fifteen times during those semesters, because I was lazy and thickheaded. So I had Mr. Hendricks, who'd already failed me once before, for a double period every day. And I almost couldn't believe it when he gave students the okay to wear that FREE SPENELLI! shirt in place of the gold Carver High gym top, after a Hillsboro kid had asked him.

"I don't care what kind of T-shirt anybody wears as long as it's clean. That's my new policy," said Hendricks, who'd lived in Hillsboro all his life. "I don't find this one offensive. That's just what some people in my community think. It's an opinion. A few states down South still fly the Confederate flag over their capitol building."

I would have called Hendricks a racist to his face, but I needed to graduate on time.

There were nearly one hundred and twenty kids in those two gym classes combined, and one of them turned out to be Charlie Scat's cousin, Spanky.

Spanky was built short and squat, and his head sat

square on his shoulders, like he didn't have any neck at all. Except for the extra weight that Scat carried, there wasn't much difference between them. And I could have picked those two out of a crowd as being related.

Hendricks had set up a batting cage in the corner of the gym and was pitching softballs underhand to kids. Everybody had to take six swings apiece.

He'd made me and Bonds go into the closet and drag out two big canvas bags. When I heard the bats rattling inside of them, I tensed up supertight.

"I'll take ten of you over here at a time, till everyone's had a chance to hit," Hendricks announced.

When my group got called over, I stayed clear of every white kid with a bat in his hands taking practice swings.

I was supposed to hit next, and Bonds was waiting right behind me.

That's when Spanky crashed our group, grabbing a metal bat with the letters R-E-S-P-O-N-S-E across the barrel, just like the one I got jumped with.

But Hendricks never asked Spanky what he was doing, and he never told him to leave.

"Come on, Teach. Lay a few watermelons over the plate for me," said Spanky, tapping the bottom of both his shoes with the bat.

Hendricks just smiled wide, lobbing one in.

Then, as he nailed the first pitch, Spanky said, "Jamel,"
like he was cracking somebody's skull.

"Jammal," he grunted as the next ball exploded off
his bat.

Bonds got up closer behind me and I could feel his hot
breath on my neck.

Hendricks let go of another pitch with an easy motion.

"Kareem of wheat," said Spanky through the ping of
the ball off the bat.

I squeezed the bat I was holding, thinking I could
choke the life out of him.

He smacked another one, calling out, "Tyrone."

"Tyree." He grinned on the next.

Then Spanky smacked one last pitch, and said,
"Tylenol—or whatever made-up medicine-chest names
their mamas give 'em."

I wanted to really thump his ass. So did every other
black kid who was listening, I could tell.

"You're up next, Jackson!" barked Hendricks.

"Here, man. Try this one for size." Spanky smirked,
shoving the bat at me.

I wasn't about to back down from that bastard. So I
dropped the bat I'd been holding. Then I grabbed the one
from his hands, and could feel the heat in it.

"Show him, Noah," said Bonds. "Show him how we play East Franklin cracker ball."

Then some other kids from my hood started trash-talking, too.

"Yeah, yeah, cracker ball, Noah!"

"Rip a few Jimmys and Tommys!"

"Whack a fat cousin Charlie!"

I set myself at the plate and took a fierce practice swing.

I could feel my mouth go bone-dry as Hendricks pulled his arm back.

"You got nothin'," said Spanky, low.

Hendricks's pitch floated up high in front of me.

I set my feet and swung with all my might. But the pitch fell a half foot short of the plate. I hit nothing but air, and my arms wound up like a corkscrew with the bat nailing me hard in the back of the head.

For a few seconds, I saw stars. And when I started to stagger, Bonds rushed in to hold me up straight.

I heard Hendricks and Spanky laughing out loud.

"That's the way it's gonna go for you in court against my cousin, Jackson," laughed Spanky. "A big swing and a miss."

I changed my clothes in the locker room with every black face looking at me like I'd let them down. And that's exactly how I felt, with a headache that pounded nonstop for the next couple of days to remind me.

Two weeks later, I walked through our apartment door after school, and Mom had a serious look on her face. A grand jury had indicted Scaturro and Spenelli on hate-crime charges a few days before, but now the pressure was going to be building on me.

"The DA called today, Noah," she said. "The trial date's set for three months from now, right around Christmas. But they say they need to start prepping you on all the questions you're gonna hear and the answers you need to give on the witness stand."

"Oh, yeah?" I asked, my voice fading low. "What if those dudes just cop a plea?"

I guess she saw my shoulders shrinking under that weight.

"All you need to do is tell the truth," Mom answered. "Then nothing can touch you. No matter what kind of mud the lawyers for the other side think they're gonna throw."

I didn't know if I believed that or not. I just knew I was tired of getting trapped in lies, like the ones I'd fed my family and Deshawna the night I went into Hillsboro.

"And part of that *truth* is you need to do a lot of self-reflection, Noah," Mom said, the anger building up in her voice. "Outside of these walls, I won't give those racists a thing to hold against you. But your father and grand-mother, and me—we don't understand how it was you couldn't tell right from wrong the night this all happened."

I knew it was coming. That I'd gotten off light for a while because of my skull. But when Mom finally let loose what she'd been holding back, I felt two inches tall stand-ing in front of her.

"I know it," I said.

"Is that what you want to teach your daughter?" she asked.

"No," I answered, feeling even smaller.

"Because if it is, you didn't learn a thing from us. Maybe we should have let the streets raise you up. That's what people will think anyway by your actions. I should have saved myself the trouble," Mom kept on. "The shame of it, a common car thief."

The DA's office set up meeting times around my school schedule, but they didn't give a shit about me missing hours at Mickey D's. I never figured that pointing a finger at those racist bastards was going to put me in the poor-house and make me half a deadbeat with Deshawna and her dad.

I complained about it. But one of the city's lawyers

told me over the phone, "We can't worry over your work hours, Noah. It's insignificant compared to this. You need to see what you're going to face in court."

He could say what he wanted, but I knew he was collecting a paycheck much fatter than mine for just being there.

My father used his vacations days with the transit authority and came along with me to every meeting.

"I don't trust anybody. Period," Dad said. "You don't know enough about life yet to challenge what they tell you as true. I wanna make sure you don't become their *boy*, 'cause you was *mine* first."

The meetings were held at a downtown office building, with five city lawyers playing different roles to get me used to the feel of a real courtroom.

They had a black woman lawyer, wearing sheer stockings and a skirt just over her knees, playing the part of Scaturro's mouthpiece. She hooked my eye, smiling easy, and then she ripped off a bunch of stinging questions.

"How many times have you been arrested?"

"What were the charges?"

"Had you ever stolen a car before and sold it to a chop shop?"

"When did you decide to take up that illegal business?"

I looked down at the floor and could hear the same snap in her voice as Mom's.

"Eyes up, Noah," another lawyer coached me. "You look like *you're* on trial here, and that's what the opposition wants."

I was sweating up a storm trying to answer everything right, and they told me not to drink any water the next time before we practiced.

"Excuse me. But the other side's gonna have a pretty lady lawyer like this one knocking me down?" I asked.

"Aaron Chapman's the opposing counsel, Noah," said one of the lawyers. "He's an overweight white man with an appetite for chewing up witnesses and spitting them across the courtroom."

"See, Noah, I grew up in East Franklin with a mother and grandmother, too," said the lady lawyer. "I know what kind of heat you're probably used to catching from *them*. That's a good start in standing up to a grilling in court. You just need to become better prepared."

There were four practice sessions altogether. And by the end of the second one, I was speaking slow and steady without using any street slang, and I was looking the lawyers, who were sitting off to the side playing the part of the jury, in their eyes at the end of every answer that mattered.

Dad didn't say much in those meetings, but when he did he made sure the lawyers heard him.

He said things like, "Calling my son a victim makes

him sound weak. Don't tell him not to stare too much at Scaturro. He's got every right. Noah was the one who got beat, not any of you."

I was just starting to trust those lawyers a little.

Then after our last session, we were waiting in the hall for the elevator. The doors opened wide and that Rao kid and his detective father stepped out. The lawyer who was bringing them upstairs knew right away he'd fucked up, and he got in between us all fast.

"Nice to see your son when him and his racist friends aren't trying to beat the black off one of us," Dad said loud and strong for Rao's father and everybody else to hear. "He learn that from the stories you told him about policing this city?"

Rao and his father both dropped their heads, and Dad's words were still echoing in that hallway after the two of them were hustled into an office.

I could feel a fire starting in my belly at having to see those bastards. But my father seemed to just shake off whatever he was feeling.

"Not a word about this to your mother," he told me on the elevator ride down. "She don't need to lose another night's sleep out of frustration."

I agreed with him and wished it could be like that for me.

We always took the subway home from the DA's office

together. My father would flash his conductor's badge and ride for free. Anytime I ever rode the trains with him before that, he'd pull me through the iron gates right behind him, without paying. But he wouldn't do it now.

"You *sure*?" I'd asked, looking to save money.

"We don't need for some cop to stop us and have the newspapers call us crooks over two dollars," he'd tell me. "So just reach your hand into your pocket and pay the fare."

After that last meeting, Dad saw one of his conductor friends working the doors from a little compartment on the train we were riding.

"I thought you was on vacation?" said the man, turning up both his palms.

"This *is* my vacation, brother," Dad said, getting up and walking over to him. "Trouble is, it's the same as work."

Then he pointed back at me. I couldn't hear what he was telling that conductor over the noise of the train. But the man nodded his head to me, and I nodded back.

I didn't know what my father could have said about me besides, *That's my son sitting there.*

I didn't know if my father was proud of me or not.

All I'd really ever done with my life is get a girl pregnant, and made the news for thinking about swiping a car and getting my ass whipped with a baseball bat.

The train made its two stops in Hillsboro, barreling out of the black tunnel into the lighted station both times. And Dad never took his eyes off me as it did, from where he was standing by his friend.

Mostly everybody who was white in our car had got off.

There was a black woman sitting across from me, about the same age as Grandma. She had two big shopping bags at her feet, and I was thinking how maybe she didn't have any family to help her. Then my eyes hooked up with hers and she put a death grip on her pocketbook.

That felt like getting kicked in the teeth by my own kind.

The train started slowing down for the first East Franklin station. I stood up, grabbing on to the handrail and getting my legs steady. Only my father didn't need to hold on to anything. He bounced along with that train, shifting his weight like he'd grown up balancing on a high wire.

"You ride enough years, you get a sense of what's coming down the line," he said after I asked him about it.

We got to our apartment door, and Destiny Love's baby stroller was folded up in the hall.

I could hear Deshawna's voice laughing from inside.

Pops counted out seventy-something dollars quick, pushing it at me.

"Here, you take care of your *business* and then some with that," he said, before turning the brass knob. "Keep your baby's mother happy."

Mom, Grandma, and Deshawna were almost having a party in there, calling out Destiny Love's name. It was the first day she'd started crawling for real. They were all trying to get her to come to them. But as soon as I stepped inside, my daughter scooted straight over to me.

DA'S OFFICE

In a windowless office, the lead lawyer sits behind a desk, stabbing his blotter with the point of a pen. The subordinate is standing with his head bowed and heels together. Directly behind the subordinate is a smoky glass door with the backward lettering of lead lawyer's name stenciled on it.

LEAD LAWYER: Honestly, do you have your head up your ass, Pierce, or what? (*Irately.*) You schedule a session with a cooperating witness who took part in the alleged attack five minutes after the victim's meeting ends! Did you think what could have happened if they met in the men's restroom and not in the hallway? You could have caused serious headlines and put a major dent in this thing by being sloppy and stupid. Screw up like that again and all you'll be prosecuting in this city are jaywalking cases. Understand me?

SUBORDINATE (*Eyes on the floor.*): Yes, sir.

LEAD LAWYER (*Still seething.*): You control your surroundings! They don't control you! And that goes for your witnesses. You'll tell them who to be, how to be, and when to be! Do you understand me, Mr. Pierce?

SUBORDINATE: I do, sir. (*His voice cracks.*)

LEAD LAWYER: It's like I've taught you almost nothing.

Chapter **SIX**

MUNCH HAD BEEN ALL OVER MY CASE ABOUT missing shifts at Mickey D's. So when I showed up for work two minutes late one Saturday, there was already another kid standing at my station, on the deep fryer.

"Jackson, see me in my office!" hollered Munch.

It wasn't anything close to being an office. It was just a big walk-in supply closet stacked to the ceiling with cartons of paper napkins and floor cleaner.

"Get into this," he said with a straight face, handing me a clown suit.

"Do what?" I said, shocked.

"I need you to put this on and give out balloons to kids," he came back. "The guy I hired to do it called in sick."

There was a curly red wig, baggy yellow pants, and floppy shoes that were five times bigger than my feet.

I stared into the whites of his eyes, like he'd lost his mind.

"Listen up, Jackson," he snapped. "Either put this outfit on or go home."

"Out of all these kids workin' here, how come me?" I asked, ready to blow.

"'Cause I'm the boss and you're the horse," he answered, snide. "That simple."

I should have walked out of there cold. But I thought about what my father would say to me if I had to borrow another day's pay, or worse, got my ass fired. Then I thought about all the things my baby daughter needed, and how Deshawna would give me grief, too.

On the flip side, I'd be embarrassed as shit for Dad or Deshawna to even see me dressed up that way. I guessed only Destiny Love would have smiled over it.

Finally, Munch just shoved that clown suit into my arms, putting a tube of white makeup on top of it. Then he walked off grinning from ear to ear. That bastard wanted me to paint my face white, like the clown in Mickey D's commercials.

I stood there steaming.

Inside the bathroom, I put that suit on over my clothes, grilling myself hard in the mirror. Then I squeezed the white makeup onto the tips of two fingers. But I couldn't rub it in, and washed my hand in the sink till the water got so hot it almost burned.

I hid my face from Munch behind a bunch of balloons, and stood outside the store for nearly four hours, trying my best to laugh and joke with every little kid who came past. No matter what color.

And I learned that as long as I was dressed as a clown and was there to *amuse* them, even white folks from Hillsboro would send their kids up to me for a free balloon.

But towards the end of my shift, Munch marched outside all pissed off.

"People are complainin', Jackson," he said. "They want to know when our clown turned *black*. What happened to the makeup I gave you?"

"What people?" I asked, staring him in the face. "Who do *they* all look like? *You?*"

Munch didn't answer. He just stormed back inside the store.

When my shift was over, I folded that clown suit up neat, making the corners sharp like it had just come out of the box. Then I left it sitting on a tabletop by the time clock. I'd sent that tube of makeup to where nobody would reach for it, burying it at the bottom of the bathroom trash beneath the sole of my shoe.

If Munch ever wanted to press me on it, he could take whatever that makeup cost out of my pay, and I wouldn't argue a lick.

The DA's office had been prepping Asa and Bonds, too. Only they never had us all down there at the same time, probably so Scat's lawyer couldn't say we worked up a story together. But we'd talk things over plenty in the cafeteria at school, like how Asa wanted to climb up into that black lady lawyer's skirt.

"A brother needs a sexy sister with a job like that," crowed Asa. "Think of all the trouble she could spring you out of."

"How she look at you?" Bonds asked him.

"Like a prince. No, check that—like a strong African king," Asa answered.

"That's how she looks at me. And I'll bet she's even nicer to Noah," said Bonds. "Know why? That's the law game—keep the witnesses walking around with a hard-on, so we'll say what they want. She probably smiles at that Rao cat, too."

"I don't know," I argued, stabbing at a dried-out slab of cafeteria meat loaf with a spork. "She seemed *real*, and representin' from East Franklin."

"Yeah? She tell you that she had a date with Rao and *his* father, right after you and *your* pops?" Bonds asked. "Or did you catch her on the sly?"

"Sister done two-time me with the wrong dude,"

sparked Asa. "I get the chance now, I'll just do her and bounce."

"What chance you got, car thief?" Bonds laughed.

"Better than you, Slim Jim," Asa said. "Least I got wire-cuttin' skills, and a GED that's coming."

"You bragging on a *GED*?" cracked Bonds.

"When you flunk your last few classes, you'll be going for one, too. Only you'll be a year behind me," said Asa. "And the new test is hard."

I listened to all that crap, looking at the rows of mostly solid black or white tables, including ours. And I wondered how much we really learned from everything that went down. We were still slinging the same old shit at each other, getting older and further behind the eight ball every day.

After more than a month of school, all the drama over that T-shirt had mostly died down. But every day I'd see at least one or two kids still wearing it.

Then one day, in Mr. Dowling's social-studies class, there was a "Do Now" question up on the board—HOW WOULD LIVING IN AMERICA BE DIFFERENT IF EVERYBODY WAS THE SAME?

"Do you mean if everybody was white?" a girl from Hillsboro asked.

"Nah, if everybody was black," somebody shot back from the other side of the room. "Right, Mr. D?"

Dowling just shook his head and answered, "Try your best with this one on your own. No direction yet from me."

I wasn't sure what to write. But all around me, for something like four or five minutes straight, I never heard so many pens flying across papers. A couple of kids even filled up whole pages, flipping them over fast to write even more.

"Okay, who wants to read what they wrote out loud?" asked Dowling, and hands went up high in every row.

"If everybody was the same, Joe Spenelli would be home on bail right now. Why? Because people who are charged with robbery and assault get bail," a girl read all excited, with her blonde bangs hitting into her eyes on every word. "So if he got accused of doing that to someone the same color as him, it couldn't be a phony charge like a hate crime."

"Let me stop you right there, thank you," said Dowling. "Who's next?"

"If everybody was the same color—black," read a dude from East Franklin, "Noah Jackson wouldn't have a steel plate in his head. Not unless he said something about somebody's mother or—"

"Everybody's the same color in Africa," a kid cut in. "Why don't *you* all go back there?"

"'Cause white people kidnapped us here for slaves!" somebody shouted. "That's why!"

Then Dowling shushed everybody down, taking control.

"What do you mean go back to Africa? What would America be without black culture?" Dowling asked the kid who'd cut in.

"Less crime. Less welfare. No projects," he answered, counting off on his fingers.

Then a black dude waved his hand wild, like he'd shit in his drawers if Dowling didn't let him say something back.

"How about no NBA, or almost any pro sports," he blurted out as Dowling pointed to him. "No fly dancing, no rap music, no jazz, no soul music, and no soul food."

"How many people in this room have ancestors from Italy?" asked Dowling.

Almost every white kid in the room raised their hands.

"You know that Sicily's part of Italy," Dowling said. "It's so close to Africa you could almost stand on Sicily's shore and hit the northern tip of Africa with a rock. Lots of Sicilians mixed with Africans, and then spread that blood all through Italy."

"But I'm not black, not even close," said a Guido dude, sitting two seats away from me. "All I wanna know is, how come they can't be more like those kids on *The Cosby Show*. Because all I ever see in this school are the low-rent kind from *Good Times*."

If I could have got away with it, I would have leaned over and smacked that guy good to shut his mouth.

Then I looked down at my own paper.

Besides my name at the top, the only words there were: NOT NEARLY AS GOOD, BUT LESS VIOLENT.

CITY JAIL—ATTORNEY/CLIENT CONFERENCE ROOM

CHARLIE SCAT (*Wears an orange jumpsuit and slippers.*): There's no good reason I can't have bail. I'm not gonna run. How the hell can I? Everybody knows my face. I even sold my car to get you money. They think I'm gonna hitchhike to Mexico? I should be at home wearing one of those bracelets around my ankle, keeping track of me. I can't take livin' here like a fuckin' animal no more. I didn't kill nobody and eat their body parts.

AARON CHAPMAN: You're high profile, Charlie. I filed motions on it, but it's probably not going to do any good. You mean something to this city now—you're their poster boy for intolerance and they're going to keep you off the streets for as long as they can.

CHARLIE SCAT: But a different judge might have gave me bail, right? (*Slams his fist on a small plastic table.*) This is prejudice—in here. Every inmate and guard that's black wants my ass in a sling.

AARON CHAPMAN: That's the reality. Your good buddy Joe Spenelli doesn't have bail, either. And he's not accused of wielding the bat. You need to separate yourself from that now. (*Picks up a yellow legal pad.*) Let's go over the bigger points of this case again.

CHARLIE SCAT: Go 'head. One more time. (*Exhales, long and loudly.*)

AARON CHAPMAN: After Spenelli and Rao woke you up, you were still half asleep. You were leaving your house to help friends in trouble, and you didn't even know these other guys were African American. Not until you ran into them.

CHARLIE SCAT: Right.

AARON CHAPMAN: When you did see them, you were just getting out of the car to talk. As for the bat, just because it was in your car to start with doesn't mean you were the one who took it out. You might have grabbed it away from Spenelli or Rao. After all, your friends were already angry. You'd never even seen these other guys.

CHARLIE SCAT: Yeah.

AARON CHAPMAN: *If* you swung that bat, it was out of fear. It all happened so fast you're not even clear on it. Noah Jackson could have sustained injuries when he fell. You never took his shoes. You didn't remove his earring.

CHARLIE SCAT: That's right. I didn't.

AARON CHAPMAN: And that n-word. You hear it every day, don't you? White kids even call each other that sometimes, just to be hip and cool.

CHARLIE SCAT: Absolutely.

AARON CHAPMAN: Ever hear African Americans call each other that, without starting a fight?

CHARLIE SCAT: All the time. (*Pauses.*) Now what about the things I told those two freakin' detectives?

AARON CHAPMAN: That was tainted. They leaned on you. Threatened—intimidated you. Especially that black one. Nothing you said before I arrived was factual. Nothing. Ka-peesh? (*Knocks a knuckle at his own temple.*)

CHARLIE SCAT: Definitely.

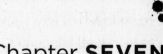

Chapter **SEVEN**

WHENEVER WE WERE AROUND SPANKY in gym, Bonds and me kept our grills set to chill, and wouldn't even think about cracking a smile. We'd both stand our ground, too, making him move over a step anytime we passed close to each other. Then one day, Bonds and Spanky wound up at the water fountain together.

I was shooting hoops at the far basket, so I didn't see it start.

"Asshole's going for water the same time as me. He puts a little hop in his step, like he's gotta get there first. I know what he's thinking—doesn't want to drink after my black lips been there. Well, I wasn't gonna suck up after his racist cracker-mouth, either," Bonds told me after school that day. "I swing my shoulders around first, right in front of him. Only he don't stop coming. So I stiffen up hard and let him bounce off me—give him a good ride, and he hits the floor."

That's when I heard kids making noise over it and saw for myself.

Spanky popped right up, but Bonds stuck his chest out and knocked him back a few feet. I thought they were about to start throwing bombs.

All my muscles tensed up, like I was standing in the middle of it myself. Not out of fear of fighting Spanky or anybody else. But from knowing that drama was about to jump off because of what happened to me that night in Hillsboro.

I was scared that feeling would follow me for the rest of my life.

Out of nowhere, Mr. Hendricks came flying in between them.

"Stop it! The two of you!" Hendricks hollered.

But he was facing Bonds and grabbed *him* by the arm, while Spanky was still looking to throw down.

Bonds yanked himself out of Hendricks's grip, to make sure Spanky didn't get in a free shot. But when he did, Hendricks's fingernails scraped a long ribbon of skin off Bonds's left forearm, from his elbow down to his wrist.

"Shiiiit!" cried Bonds, shaking his arm in the air trying to stop the sting.

Another gym teacher must have radioed for the deans and school security, and they came running on the double inside of the next minute.

In the end, the deans didn't suspend either Bonds or Spanky, because neither one of them threw a single

punch. But Bonds's mother made a real fuss to the principal about her son's scratches. The Board of Education
came down hard on Hendricks. They made him take off
three days without pay and apologize to Bonds in front of
the whole gym class.

On the first day of his suspension, Hendricks came in
to apologize, standing in front of us in his street clothes.

"It's a sad day for teachers," Hendricks said, so steamed
he was red-faced. "We're supposed to keep you all safe,
even if that means putting ourselves in the middle of
something dangerous. I put my hands on somebody here,
trying to do just that. And I'm sorry he got scratched up a
little. I was wrong, Mr. Bonds. *Forgive me.*"

Nearly every black kid there was grinning wide to
hear Hendricks eat crow like that, and have him call
Bonds "Mister." Spanky and the kids he hung tight with
were either staring at the high ceiling or the wooden
boards in the gym floor. But there were plenty of white
kids who hated Hendricks—kids he'd nailed with a
dodgeball or barked on for not being strong enough to
climb the thirty-foot ropes. And they were all enjoying
that show, too.

Hendricks was walking towards the door when he
turned back around and said, "And you can all bet that's
the last time I get involved in anything. If you twist an ankle, jam a finger—just go running to some other phys ed

instructor, or maybe the school nurse. I got a *hands-off* policy from now on."

At lunch, Bonds told Asa and me, "Yeah, it was pretty much a suck-ass apology. But I loved it anyway. Best day I ever had in school."

"I wish for anything I could have seen it," said Asa, "You gonna sue?"

"I want to, but my mother says we already got money for iodine and Band-Aids," Bonds came back. "Noah's the one about to hit it rich. Start a civil suit for money against Charlie Scat—the way those people did on O.J. Simpson."

"Yeah, right," I said. "That Scat dude owned nothing but his Land Rover, and I read where he sold that to pay for his lawyer."

"So maybe the judge will sentence him to be your butler," said Asa, cracking up. "He'll have to pick up after you in the hood. Then you'll make him bend over on the street corner, and brothers passing by can take turns booting him in the ass."

That didn't sound half bad to me.

This dime-piece of a shorty named Tiffany came over to our table and gave Bonds a high five for grounding Hendricks.

"I hate that gym teacher. I hope he gets fired and has to collect cans off the street," she said. "You got it goin' on, too, Noah. The way you're standing up to those Hillsboro thugs."

Then she gave *me* a high five and let her sweet palm sit flat against mine for more than a second.

"I'm a part of this crew. I don't get no love?" asked Asa, with his open hand out in front of him.

Tiffany just left Asa hanging, sitting herself down right next to me.

My eyes hooked up with hers and I felt a fire spark.

Bonds must have picked up on it, because he bounced right away.

But Asa's head was hard as wood, and he was still running game at her.

Then two of Deshawna's homegirls came walking past. They stopped right in front of us grilling Tiffany, like I was Deshawna's private property. So I knew that whole scene would get back to Deshawna, who had a different lunch period. Only it was sure to get blown up bigger, with them telling it like Tiffany was sitting in my lap.

Halloween fell on a Friday, and I worked the late shift that night at Mickey D's. I left the place around midnight, walking home alone through no-man's-land with all that Halloween craziness in the streets. Junior high school kids were really feeling it, throwing eggs, chasing each other with cans of shaving cream, and swinging sweat socks filled with flour.

I guess I looked like an adult to them, because they all just ran right past me, like I was too old to be a target in that game.

I remembered crossing Decatur on Halloween with my friends when I was that age. We wore masks that covered up our faces, and went trick-or-treating on the first few blocks into Hillsboro. Those were all private houses, and the people who lived there could afford to give out brand-name mini–candy bars—Three Musketeers, Snickers, Almond Joy—the works.

"Trick or treat," we'd say, with a high pitch to it.

We were trying to make our voices sound white, like there really was such a thing. Then we'd take our haul back to East Franklin, wanting to curse out the people from around our way who gave us loose pieces of candy corn or one-penny bubble gums.

This was my weekend to have Destiny Love, and that next day I took her to the playground with Mom and Grandma.

"Look at this place," Mom said, disgusted. "Eggs everywhere."

"Don't these young hooligans know it's a sin to waste food? What do their families teach them?" asked Grandma. "Noah, did you ever disgrace your own neighborhood like this, growing up?"

"No, Grandma," I answered, knowing I'd boosted plenty of eggs from our refrigerator to chuck on Halloween.

But I was starting to see things different now.

I sat Destiny Love on my lap and went back and forth slow on the real swings, holding on to her with one hand and the steel chain with the other.

She let out a squeal of pure joy every time we swung in either direction.

And a good part of me felt that inside again, too—like I was still a kid.

That was the kind of thing my daughter could bring to me.

When we finished, I was super careful where I let Destiny Love crawl in that park, not wanting any of that filth on the ground to touch her.

DESHAWNA'S APARTMENT

DESHAWNA: I hear you, Tamika! I'll torch his cheating ass! (*Slams down the phone.*)

DESHAWNA'S DAD: What's all that noise about, Deshawna? (*Muffles his anger.*) You're gonna wake up your daughter.

DESHAWNA: Noah Jackson thinks he's God's gift—

that's what, sending out signals to every girl at school. All my friends *know* he's playing me.

DESHAWNA'S DAD: And what do you think he was after when he got you pregnant? A seventeen-year-old boy's mind is on but one thing. Having a child with you ain't gonna change that so fast. That's just the truth of it, little girl.

DESHAWNA: Noah's no closer to putting a ring on my finger than the day I had his baby.

DESHAWNA'S DAD: I told you ten times already. Now I'll tell you again—just 'cause you share blood together, that don't make you family.

DESHAWNA: Sometimes I really love him, Daddy. When they busted his skull with that bat, and I thought he was gonna die (*Starts to cry.*), I couldn't take it.

DESHAWNA'S DAD: You don't know real love for a man yet. You just concentrate on loving that baby of yours. What I had for your mama, that was real love. (*Hugs Deshawna tight.*) I held her in my arms for the last two months of her life while that damn diabetes broke down all her functions. You need to go through hard times together to find out what love is.

DESHAWNA (*Through a flood of tears.*): I miss Mama so much. I wish she could have seen Destiny Love.

DESHAWNA'S DAD (*Softly.*): We both do, baby. We both do.

DESHAWNA: What am I gonna do about Noah?

DESHAWNA'S DAD: That boy comes from decent folks. No matter what happens between you and him, he might grow up to be a good father. That's all you can hope for now. That's all you can try to hold him to.

Chapter EIGHT

WE FOUGHT FOR ALMOST FIFTEEN MINUTES with Deshawna pressing me about Tiffany.

"When you want me to be your wifey, I am, and when you don't, I just disappear from your head," she complained, with our daughter asleep in her stroller as we started a second lap around my block.

"I was just sitting there. I can't help it if shorties come on to *me*," I said. "I didn't do anything with her and you're still on my case. How's that right?"

"It's not what you don't do, Noah," Deshawna said. "It's the respect you need to show me in front of people. The same way I'm always going shopping for Pampers and baby clothes alone. It don't matter that you give me money. You think your time's more important than mine."

"Yeah, I see how it's all my problem," I said, short and sarcastic.

I turned my face away from her, before I boiled over and said something too strong. As we turned the corner, Destiny Love woke up, letting out a loud cry.

Deshawna and me both went to reach for her, and nearly knocked heads.

So I took a step back and said, "I'm sorry. All right? I know I'm not perfect."

"That's all I wanted to hear," she said, picking up our daughter in her arms.

Later that week, I got my first-semester report card at school. I knew I was doing all right but my eyes skimmed it quick anyway just to make sure there were no red marks. Then I took a look for real and almost couldn't believe it. Mr. Dowling gave me a 95 and his handwritten comment next to the grade read—*Noah, you're learning more about social studies through your personal trials than I could ever teach you.*

Reading that started a real feeling of pride churning inside of me—something I hadn't felt about myself in a long time.

I got an 85 in math, and Hendricks gave me an "S" for "satisfactory" in both of my PE classes. I had a GPA of 90, nearly fifteen points higher that it had ever been before.

On my first open period, I met with my guidance counselor, to fill out the paperwork to enroll in a city college next semester. I even checked off "engineering" as the major that I was most interested in.

When I was in the fifth grade, some kid's uncle who

was an engineer came in to talk to us for career day. He was black, acted supercool, and wore the sharpest alligator shoes I'd ever seen. I remember how he walked over to our classroom bulletin board and pointed to our math tests hanging up there.

"All of these students with the one hundred percents on their math papers—they're heading in right direction to become engineers," he said before he called out six or seven names off the tops of those tests, including mine.

Then he showed us a tape of skyscrapers and big bridges swaying in the wind, and explained to us how an engineer designed them so they wouldn't crack or buckle from the strain.

Anytime after that, whenever somebody asked me what I wanted to be and wouldn't settle for answers like a millionaire or a pro football player, I'd say, "An engineer."

"An engineer on a *train* maybe," Dad would rag on me whenever I talked about college during my junior and first senior year. "Every father wants something better for his son, Noah. But a degree in engineering is just crazy talk, unless you're finally ready to get serious about school."

It hurt my pride every time Dad poked at me like that. But I never really argued back too hard, because I knew he was right.

All that afternoon at Mickey D's I could feel my chest pumped up, standing at my station in front of the deep fryer. It didn't matter what kind of shit Munch threw my way. None of it could touch me. I kept pulling that report card out of my back pocket, reading Dowling's comment to myself over and over. And I left there for home thinking, *Destiny Love's daddy is going to be somebody.*

For a change, nearly every part of me was feeling whole. The patch of hair the doctors cut out of my scalp had grown completely back in, and the headaches I was having had mostly disappeared.

I bounced through the front door ready to show off my report card, but nobody there was in a mood to celebrate.

They were all raging over the TV news, and I felt like I'd just been sucker punched walking into my own house.

"Two years!" Mom hollered. "Two miserable years! That's what they think taking a bat to my boy's head is worth!"

Every nerve inside of me pulled tight.

"Outrageous! That's no justice at all," shrieked Grandma.

At first, I thought they were screaming about Charlie Scat.

But they weren't.

It was Spenelli.

He'd come clean, copping a plea bargain with the city.

"Why didn't the prosecutors call here first and ask *Noah* if that was enough time?" ranted my father, pointing his finger at me.

He was looking for an answer. But I didn't have one.

"You can't trust *any* of 'em!" Dad steamed. "Even them black lawyers are just carrying their white bosses' bags. They got no real power!"

That wasn't all the news.

The prosecutors *officially* decided to let Rao walk in exchange for testifying.

The face of that white detective who talked to me in the hospital—the one who swore it would never happen— burned inside my brain. And except for Charlie Scat, I started to hate him the most, blaming him for everything I felt cheated out of that night.

The next day, in a hallway at school, I heard a mob of voices shouting, "Guilty!"

A girl wearing a FREE SPENELLI! T-shirt was walking as fast as she could, heading in my direction. She pressed her books tight to her chest, almost completely covering up the words on that shirt. And she was staring straight down, with tears streaming from her eyes.

The hallways were packed and nearly every black face she passed roared out, "Guilty!" too.

Then a sister ran up to her and said, "Take off that damn shirt. He already admitted what he done."

I didn't say anything to that girl with the shirt.

I didn't have to. That bastard Spenelli said it all when he copped to those charges. For those few seconds it didn't matter to me that he only got two years. It only mattered that he'd confessed to what he was.

I just listened to that chant of "Guilty!"echoing through the hall.

Not a single white kid opened their mouth to stick up for Spenelli, or for her wearing that shirt. And after that, I never saw one of those shirts around school again.

Parent/teacher conferences were that same night. Dad had to work late, but I went along with Mom and Grandma, ready to catch some real praise for my grades. I'd taken enough hits in the past over low marks that I really wanted to be there this time.

"Forget physical education," I told them. "All that racist from Hillsboro—Hendricks—can tell you about me is that I come prepared every day now."

"Well, I don't need to hear that from *him*," said Mom. "*I'm* the one who washes out your gym clothes every night."

So I took them straight upstairs to the second floor to see Mr. Dowling.

We had to wait fifteen minutes while Dowling finished his conference with another family. He was ripping into some kid who wasn't even there, calling him "unmotivated" and "lazy." And I knew that would build *me* up even more.

Grandma walked around the classroom reading the posters on every wall.

"Noah Jackson, introduce me to your family," Dowling finally said, reaching out to shake Mom's hand.

"Mr. Dowling, this is my mother, Mrs. Jackson, and that's my grandmother," I said, loud and proper.

"I'm *also* Mrs. Jackson," announced Grandma. "I've been looking at your poster of Harriet Tubman and the Underground Railroad. It's so moving. I want you to know that I'm only three generations removed from slavery. My great-grandfather was—"

That's when her voice faded to almost nothing.

"Are you all right?" Mom asked her.

"Here, sit down, Mrs. Jackson," said Dowling.

But before anybody could get Grandma into a chair, she collapsed to the floor.

"Lord Jesus, help her!" screamed Mom.

Mr. Dowling got on the intercom, calling the main

office. Then he whipped out a cell phone and dialed 911.

Grandma started breathing hard, like she was in a race.

She was gasping for air—*Huh, huh, huh.*

Then she stopped cold and I thought she'd quit breathing for good.

Every emotion inside me was spinning out of control, running wild with nowhere to go. It all built up super-fast with Mom's hysterical screams echoing through my skull.

I looked into Grandma's face.

Her brown eyes were open wide.

And I nearly sprinted out of my shoes, flying through the hallway.

I didn't know where I was headed or if I was running out of pure fear.

I shot down the stairs, taking them two at a time.

Then I hit the first floor and found my voice.

"Help us!" I hollered. "We need a doctor! Help!"

People were pouring out of every room, but I streaked past them all towards the gym. I guess I'd gone there on instinct.

"Dowling's class! Hurry!" I yelled, running into the gym office.

But Hendricks was the only PE teacher inside.

He looked me straight in the eye, and for a second I swore there wasn't anyone else in the whole world except him and me.

I ran back to Dowling's class, exhausted, pushing myself to keep up close on Hendricks's heels.

I got there right behind him, and saw Hendricks take a long look at Grandma stretched out on the floor. He kneeled down next to her, doubling up his palms on top of her chest, pushing down, again and again.

And what suddenly jumped into my brain was that speech Hendricks gave about his new "hands-off" policy.

Then Hendricks put his lips over Grandma's, giving her two long breaths.

Mom buried her head into my chest, crying, "Lord, don't take her!"

But my eyes were glued on them.

Hendricks kept repeating that CPR cycle. Finally, he checked Grandma's pulse, and then backed away, giving her room to breathe.

EMS workers came charging into the class with all of their equipment.

Then I watched Hendricks wipe his mouth off on the sleeve of his shirt, before he walked away without saying a word.

I didn't know if I wanted to run him down and hug

him tight for what he did, or if I wanted to wrap both my hands around his throat and strangle the life out of him for who he really was.

Grandma was conscious again before the EMS workers carried her down the stairs on a stretcher.

"Stop fussing over me this way," she said in a weak voice. "I'm all right now."

I called my father on his cell phone to let him know that we were heading to the hospital. But his train must have been deep underground, because he didn't pick up and I had to leave a message.

"It's me. Grandma got sick! She passed out at my school and we're going with her in the ambulance to . . . *Mister*, where we going? . . . East Franklin Memorial. Get there as quick as you can, Dad! Please!"

The whole ride to the hospital, Grandma was squeezing Mom's hand with more and more strength.

"You had us so worried," Mom told her, between a smile and a cry. "You're not allowed to do that to your family. Right, Noah?"

My insides had nearly gone numb. But without Dad around I knew I had to step up and act the man. And not be some scared kid.

"I'm the one who studied to get those good grades," I teased her, raising my voice over the siren. "But it's Grandma getting all this attention tonight."

Grandma's mouth and nose were covered by an oxygen mask, so she just shifted her eyes between Mom and me.

I could feel the vibrations from every bump and pothole we hit in the street.

And every time I shut my eyes to pray, all I could see was that scene with Hendricks breathing life back into Grandma.

The doctors in the emergency room told us that Grandma had suffered a heart attack.

"She's very lucky. Whoever administered CPR probably saved her life," said a black doctor in a white lab coat. "But there's more to be done here. We need to perform a procedure where we reopen the blood vessels to the heart by inserting a tiny balloon."

Mom's hands were shaking as she signed all the paperwork, and they took Grandma upstairs to get ready. I put both my hands on Mom's shoulders to hold her steady. But I kept looking behind me, too, praying that my father would show up soon.

PROTECTIVE CUSTODY RECREATION YARD/ CITY JAIL

A small cement courtyard surrounded on all sides by the jail is broken up into four fenced-off rectangles where groups of inmates exercise. Each rectangle has a basketball hoop, and there is a

*walkway between divisions for corrections officers
to monitor the recreation activities. Charlie Scat
occupies a rectangle with two other inmates—one
black and one white. In the rectangle to Scat's right
exercises a lone black inmate.*

CHARLIE SCAT: (*Paces the perimeter of his rectangle.*) Locked down alone for twenty-three hours a
day with one stinking exercise period. Hoo-fuckin'-
ray for me.

BLACK INMATE #1 (*From the rectangle to Scat's
right.*): Hey, you—Fatty-Vanilla Donut. What you in
for? Boosting Krispy Kremes?

CHARLIE SCAT: Maybe I'm a mafia don, Buckwheat.
(*Continues to pace.*)

WHITE OFFICER (*To Black Inmate #1.*): You don't
know who that is? That's the Babe Ruth of Hillsboro.
He's got no problem playing baseball with the brothers, as long as he's cracking heads with the bat.

BLACK INMATE #1: Word. That's him? They better
keep this fence up in front of me. I'll smack the shit
out of that coward.

CHARLIE SCAT: Go mug another old lady for her
pocketbook! Then hit the pipe! (*Inhales deeply and,
holding his breath, pretends to get high.*)

VOICE (*From a barred window above.*): Suck on this, Bat-man!

BLACK INMATE #1: See, you'd be somebody's bitch if you were in population, cracker.

CHARLIE SCAT (*Loses his temper.*): Crackhead!

BLACK OFFICER: How many years you looking at, Scaturro?

CHARLIE SCAT: Twenty-five. That long enough for ya, Ace?

BLACK OFFICER: After I retire, my kids can finish watching your racist ass. (*Laughs.*)

CHARLIE SCAT (*Snidely.*): I'm not looking for years. I'm looking for justice. And that tin badge you're wearing ain't gonna get it for me.

BLACK INMATE #1 (*To Black Inmate #2, inside Scat's rectangle.*): Yo, *Black*, you gonna represent and whip this boy's ass or what?

CHARLIE SCAT: Bring it! I don't care. Just 'cause it's two on one, don't let that scare you. (*Other white inmate walks as far away from Scat as possible.*) Go ahead! Punk out! (*To white inmate.*) I got two ex-friends just like you. It's all on *me* anyway!

WHITE OFFICER (*To Black Officer.*): How long you think it's gonna take us to open that gate if something jumps off?

BLACK OFFICER: I figure at least thirty seconds. (*Grins wide.*) Maybe more.

BLACK INMATE #2 (*Inside Scat's rectangle.*): I ain't picking up another charge for killing this piece of crap. That's nothing but a setup, right there. (*Shakes his head.*) Just tell me, Fatty, how come you hate my people so much?

CHARLIE SCAT: I don't hate black people! (*Screams to the walls of the courtyard.*) I don't! I love them all! I love them so much I wanna fuck 'em! All right?

VOICE (*From a different window above.*): We don't love you, asshole! But we'll fuck you, too.

CHARLIE SCAT: Come on, man. One on one then. (*Points to the worn-out basketball in Black Inmate #2's hands.*)

BLACK INMATE #2: Here! (*Nearly knocks Scat over with a two-handed chest pass.*)

CHARLIE SCAT (*Wildly angry.*): I don't need no bat! I got *skillz.* Wanna see? Watch me! (*Scat slams the ball down to dribble, but it flies up off the concrete, nailing him hard in the chin.*)

Hysterical, howling laughter from a dozen windows and everyone else on the ground echoes through the courtyard.

CHARLIE SCAT: Fuck you all! (*Kicks the ball into the chain-link fence with a thud.*)

Chapter NINE

IT DIDN'T MATTER THAT THE DOCTORS SAID Grandma would be all right. Those few hours in that waiting room while they did a *simple procedure* felt like forever. I was wound up so tight I couldn't keep still, pacing back and forth till I memorized every magazine cover and stain on the couch cushions inside those four walls.

I looked around at all the other black faces of the patients and their families, and wondered what was the *only* difference between East Franklin Memorial, where Grandma was, and St. Luke's hospital in Hillsboro, where I got took. Was it just the neighborhoods they were in? Or did people in Hillsboro get better doctors because they owned their own houses and had more money to pay?

Then I started to wonder if I'd still be alive, or maybe some kind of brain-damaged vegetable, if I got attacked on the other side of Decatur Avenue and that ambulance had brought me here instead.

Mom was a wreck, sobbing almost the whole time.

And anybody would have believed it was *her* mother that was sick and not my father's.

Then Dad walked in and she buried her face in the shoulder of his blue conductor's shirt.

"Lord knows, this family's seen enough of hospitals in the last four months," said Dad, who had to stay with his train till it reached the end of the line after he'd got my message. "But if I could, I would have sprouted wings to get here faster."

I stood up straight, looking him in the eye.

He felt the wet patch of tears over my heart, from when I'd been holding Mom. Then Dad put his hand behind my head, pulling me in close.

By the time Thanksgiving came, Grandma was back on her feet, and to celebrate we had a big dinner at our house. Deshawna and Destiny Love were there. Deshawna's dad was invited, too. That was the first time we'd all mixed together around a holiday dinner table, like one big family.

I noticed that Deshawna's dad treated me better in front of my family than he did over at his house.

"Please pass me over those fried peas," he said, proper. "Thank you kindly, young man."

That's when I started to wonder if it was possible I could just talk to him over here on holidays and nowhere else.

Mom found an old picture book from when I was young for Destiny Love to look at. It had drawings of the pilgrims and Indians at the very first Thanksgiving. I remembered that book. When I got a little older I played cowboys and Indians, and I always wanted to be the cowboys. Then one day in sixth-grade history class it hit me how the Indians were just like black people. They got pushed off their land and shoved into places where white people didn't have to see them. After that, I never rooted for the cowboys to win again. Instead, I wanted to see them all get scalped.

"Come here, Noah," Grandma called out after dinner, with the stripped carcass of a twelve-pound turkey in the center of the table. "You and I got a right to give special thanks for still being here. I guess God's not through teaching either one of us yet. We still have lots of blessings coming our way. Now grab on to the other end of this wishbone. Pull as hard as you can. Your grandmother still has some strength left in her."

"Amen!" hollered everyone, almost all at once.

I didn't know what to wish for, and my mind couldn't focus on any one thing.

When that wishbone split in two, Grandma had the bigger half in her hand.

"Don't fret," Grandma told me. "My wish had to do with good things coming *your* way, child. With lots of understanding for people."

I needed it, too, because I didn't know how to look Mr. Hendricks in the face anymore. He kept that smug grill on all the time during PE now, like I should bend down to kiss his feet for what he did.

Everybody at school knew about him saving Grandma. And one day in the locker room, Bonds and me heard Spanky running his mouth to his friends about it.

"I hear Hendricks got himself a new housemaid," cackled Spanky, from a couple of rows of lockers away. "That's the way it works, right? You save somebody's life and they owe you. It's like they're your personal slave now."

My blood boiled inside my veins.

I slammed my locker shut, pretending Spanky's melon-head was between the door and the doorjamb.

"Better ask somebody for the address of the state pen!" barked Bonds. "You'll be visiting your fat-ass cousin there soon."

"I should be able to get it from anybody that's black," Spanky shot back. "Half their family's usually locked up."

I just kept my mouth shut and let Spanky and his whole Hillsboro crew clear out of there before I finished getting dressed.

I had to deal with it at home, too.

"I phoned your gym teacher while you were at school today. The Holy Spirit just moved me to do it," Grandma told me while I was trying to clean the mess of my clothes and Destiny Love's toys in my room. "Mr. Richard Hendricks. His private number wasn't listed, so I called him at Carver."

"W-w-why, Grandma?" I asked through a stutter.

"It's only right, Noah," she answered, short.

It took me a few minutes to get up the nerve to say what was really on my mind. But when I finally did, I let the words fly out fast so they wouldn't fall flat on my tongue.

"Don't it feel wrong to you that a racist from Hillsboro—'cause I *know* that's what he is—saved you?"

"Is that what's been eating at your insides?" she said. "Noah, no matter what the world puts on us, or what we put on other folks, we're all God's children. Black or white, or any color in the rainbow."

"Hendricks is just like those kids who split my skull with that bat," I said, charged up. "He's no better."

"Noah, you've every right to be angry. But don't let it consume you. A life is measured by the impact it has on others. I pray that one day you'll find a way to take what happened to you and shine a light on it for people to see," Grandma said. "I hate lots of things I've seen and fought against them all my life. And I wouldn't want to be standing in some folks' shoes on the Judgment Day. But it's not up to you or me to do the judging. That's for God to do. I suppose when there's no hope left for any of us, there won't be the grace of another flood. He'll send his *fire* next time to burn this world clean."

"I guess," I said, frustrated.

"All I got at your school was an answering machine. I left a message, but I know those things have a way of getting lost in a busy building like that," Grandma said, handing me a sealed envelope. "I want you to deliver this letter to Mr. Hendricks for me. Just to make sure he knows my feelings."

That night, and on the way to school the next morning, I thought about opening that envelope and reading Grandma's letter. I was worried that she was going to give Hendricks the kind of props he didn't deserve, and let him off the hook for looking down on anybody who wasn't white. Then that smug grin on his face would be set in stone forever.

Grandma had always been hard as nails against his kind. So I couldn't figure it.

I wasn't sold on everything she'd said straight off, either. I wasn't happy about leaving the judging to anybody else. I'd already seen too many big-time haters on the news get off with a puny slap on the wrist.

So maybe God wasn't watching all the time.

I didn't know if Grandma had gone soft from being so close to dying. I just knew that growing up she'd seen racist things go down a hundred times worse than I ever did.

Deep down, I had too much respect for Grandma to read her private feelings.

But I couldn't bring myself to put that letter into Hendricks's hand. So I shoved it into his mailbox inside the main office and walked as far away from it as I could.

That same day, there was a fight in the cafeteria maybe two minutes before I got there. I stepped inside and half the kids were standing in a wide circle watching security get whoever was fighting pinned down and under control.

The circle was mostly white on one side and black on the other.

It reminded me of that Chinese symbol—the yin and yang—I'd seen in martial-arts movies.

Suddenly I heard Asa's angry voice hollering, "He's a racist! Ain't nobody can tell me different, and I'd slap his ass again for what he said!"

It was Asa who'd been fighting, and I watched as security led him through the crowd with his hands cuffed behind him.

But I did a double take when I saw that the other dude in cuffs, the one Asa had been scrapping with, was black, too.

"He's a black-on-black racist!" Asa kept on. "That's worse,

because he's against his own kind! A damn traitor!"

Then Bonds found me. He said that Asa had fought some dude on the debate team because he'd done a project with a white kid, arguing that by law Charlie Scat and Spenelli should have got bail. Somehow Asa heard about it. So he snaked his way through the lunch line and jumped in that dude's face, insulting the shit out of him. But when the dude didn't back down, it was on.

I listened to that story, and after hearing it, I couldn't stomach eating a thing.

APARTMENT 3C—12TH STREET AND DUPONT AVENUE, EAST FRANKLIN

(It's 7:05 P.M. A phone inside the apartment is ringing.)

MOM (*Answers a phone on the kitchen wall.*): Jackson residence. Who's calling, please? . . . Yes, I'll get him. NOAH! TELEPHONE! (*Noah comes out of his bedroom, wiping the sleep from his eyes, still wearing his uniform from Mickey D's.*) It's one of the lawyers for the city.

NOAH (*Takes the phone.*): Hello? . . . I thought we finished those meetings? . . . I know the trial's coming in another week. But I can't miss any more time from work. They'll fire me.

DAD (*From the living room.*): I *knew* this was coming. They just tell you it's over with so they can start
you up fresh again, later. This way they don't burn you
out. But they already got *everything* they needed. I
was there.

NOAH: My father can't miss more time at work, either. . . . Because he's not gonna let me come down
there without him.

DAD (*Enters the kitchen.*): That's right.

MOM (*Grabs the phone from Noah, and snaps at
the lawyer.*): You understand we have a life here?
One with bills to stress over. Now you all have worked
very hard on Noah's behalf, and we appreciate it. But
we understand a good part of this is about *your* ca-
reers, too. That's why you probably let that Rao boy
walk—to stay in good with the police department.
And why you let that Spenelli take two lousy years
instead of going to trial, so he'd turn on his friend.
So don't pretend with us that this is all about justice
for you, because we see it's not! (*Hands the phone
back to Noah.*)

NOAH: Listen, I'll be here every night after work if
you need to call and go over things.

DAD (*To his wife.*): You were right on the money with
that speech. It needed to be said.

NOAH: I guess she's coming. I don't really know.

Why? . . . You're not worried about her crying, or making a fuss? . . . Yeah? . . . I'll see . . . All right. Good-bye. (*Hangs up the phone.*)

MOM: What was that last part about?

(*Noah, his mother, and his father are standing in a triangle, facing one another.*)

NOAH: They want to know if my daughter's coming to the trial, especially on the first day. So the jury can see her and keep a picture in their minds of what it would be like if she didn't have a daddy—if Scat would have killed me with that bat.

DAD (*In a mocking tone.*): She's a prop to them. A piece of furniture. Just to set the stage.

MOM (*Shakes her head.*): Lord, deliver us from our enemies and shield us from these lawyers.

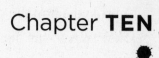

Chapter **TEN**

THE NIGHT BEFORE THE TRIAL STARTED I left my job at Mickey D's around nine o'clock. The wind was biting cold and the streets were nearly deserted. Suddenly sleet began blowing sideways and I pulled my hoodie up, knotting the string. Then I ducked my head down low to keep my face from getting slapped at.

I thought I heard something behind me.

But when I turned around it was just my own footprints swirling through that white sleet on the sidewalk, till the wind made them disappear, like I'd never been there.

That's when I decided to keep my feet facing in the opposite direction, and I started walking back through no-man's-land towards Spaghetti Park.

I guess I'd been through too much to be afraid anymore.

But I kept a sharp eye for every crack in the cement in front of me.

When I got there, the park was dark and totally empty.

I walked along the outside fence, past the swings and monkey bars to the big athletic field that connects to it.

I looked up at the telephone wire over the street to find my sneakers from that football game we'd won freshman year.

There they were, still hanging in the Crackers' Hall of Fame. And in that fierce wind, every pair of shoes up there looked like they were running.

For a while, I just watched them all going nowhere.

I knew that wasn't how I wanted my life to be—just kicking in the wind, never getting ahead to someplace worth being.

I'd made it to that goal line for a touchdown once before, with all those Armstrong High racists trying to stop me. Now I had to do it again. Only instead of holding a football, I'd be carrying something much bigger. Something for every brother and sister in East Franklin, and probably everywhere else. And especially for my baby daughter who was going to grow up around here.

So I pulled my hoodie back down and started home with my head held high, deciding I could take whatever that wind had to dish out.

The next morning, the city sent two cars to take my family and me to the courthouse. I rode in one black sedan, sandwiched in the backseat between a pair of lawyers who went over last-minute questions and answers with me.

In the car right behind us rode Dad, Mom, Grandma, Deshawna, and Destiny Love.

"Men aren't born. They're made. Remember that," my father told me before we left the house.

"Yeah? How long does it take?" I asked him.

"I'll let you know, son," he answered. "When I find out, I'll let you know."

Those were the words ringing in my ears, not anything those lawyers were saying.

Standing on the highway overpass was an old man covered from head to toe in American flags. He had his jacket collar turned up, gloves on his hands, and huge oversize sunglasses that nearly blocked out his face, making it hard to tell what color his skin was.

He just kept waving those flags for everybody stuck in traffic.

It was funny to see him, but it wasn't like a joke.

He looked serious about it.

It made me think of the times in the first grade when I stressed over getting the words to the Pledge of

Allegiance right. How I was about to put my hand on a Bible in court now, swearing to tell the truth. And how I would probably hear Scat do the same.

Both of those lawyers were still talking at me, looking at long yellow notepads in their laps. So I don't think either one of them even noticed that old man up there, as we inched our way underneath him.

In the courtroom, I sat with the city lawyers at a big oak table. My family was in the first row of seats, right behind us. Farther back, my social-studies teacher, Mr. Dowling, was there, too.

There were mostly black folks in the rows of seats on our side, with white people from Hillsboro, including Scat's mother and his cousin Spanky, on the other. And it reminded me of how the cafeteria tables at Carver usually filled up.

Most of the white people there in court had the same look on their faces—like they'd just spit at us when nobody was watching and were mad as hell that we even thought they might have done it.

Only I didn't want to turn the other cheek. I wanted to spit back on all of *them*, with their eyes right on me.

"Garbage. That's all this is. A setup by the politicians," I could hear Scat's mother telling the people around her, and all of them agreeing.

Then I saw her try to eyeball Mom.

"Our sons all bleed the same blood," Mom said, loud enough for her to hear.

"Lord, you know that's true," echoed Grandma.

That's when two court officers brought Charlie Scat in through a side door. And even with his hands cuffed behind him, my heart jumped, like he was coming at me swinging that bat all over again.

The officers undid his cuffs, and Scat kissed his mother on the cheek.

"Let's hope we get justice today," he told her.

That was the first time I'd heard his voice since he'd screamed "Nigger" at me.

Then he tugged at his shirt collar and tie, and sat down staring straight ahead, like I wasn't even there.

His lawyer, Aaron Chapman, unbuckled his briefcase and the *pop* echoed through the courtroom.

"All rise!" shouted a court officer.

The sound of my heart beating got covered up for a second by shuffling feet and chairs sliding back.

The judge was white and wore a long black robe that touched the floor.

"The People versus Charles Scaturro," another officer announced.

I wondered exactly who those "people" were. I wanted to know how many of them were from East Franklin and how many were from Hillsboro.

The jury came inside. Seven of them were black and five were white, with three alternate jurors behind them in case anybody got sick or something.

My lawyer was the first one to speak.

"Ladies and gentlemen of the jury, the facts here are simple and undeniable," he started out. "On the night of August ninth, Noah Jackson, Asa Jenkins, and Robert Bonds entered the community of Hillsboro, on foot, with the idea of stealing a car. But they never actually did. The defendant, Charles Scaturro, and two accomplices, Thomas Rao and Joseph Spenelli, saw the trio of African Americans in their neighborhood, with absolutely no knowledge of their plan. Then, solely because their race, Scaturro and his two accomplices, including Thomas Rao, who will later his testify to this, chased down these three men while hurling epithets at them. And when Noah Jackson tripped to the ground, Scaturro slammed him in the head with an aluminum baseball bat, fracturing Mr. Jackson's skull. That *hate crime*, that racially motivated attack, severely jeopardized the life of this student, son, and young father to an infant girl."

Most of the juror's eyes turned towards Destiny Love, who was sitting on Deshawna's lap.

My eyes went to her, too.

But I didn't bring my baby daughter for the jury to peep.

In my mind, she wasn't anybody's prop.

I'd talked it over with Deshawna. I'd brought Destiny Love there for one reason—I wanted to be able to tell her one day that she was sitting in that courtroom watching when her father finally stood up for himself in front of everybody.

"My daughter and I both want to see that," Deshawna had said.

The trial lasted for another three days, and everybody in court heard from Aaron Chapman all about those two times I'd been nabbed by the cops. And how Asa had just got arrested at school for starting a fight. They heard it even though the city lawyers objected, saying it had nothing to do with this case.

"I'll allow it," said the judge.

Chapman would ask me questions about those arrests on cross-examination, and all the time he was talking, I'd look at his big white horse teeth, past his gums and straight down his throat, knowing I wasn't about to let him chew me up.

"You make mistakes when you're young," I answered from the witness stand. "I've made some. But that's all behind me now."

I had to look at pictures of myself with my skull split open, and of my cell phone covered in my blood. My hands were sweating as I held those photos, and the feeling left my fingertips. I looked right over at Charlie Scat, too. But he wouldn't let his eyes come anywhere close to meeting mine.

When Rao came in, people sitting behind Scat's side let him have it good.

"Rat! Where's your cheese? Better find someplace new to live!"

That's when the judge pounded his gavel, screaming, "I'll clear this courtroom, and hold the perpetrators in contempt if I hear another word directed towards the witness!"

Charlie Scat stared Rao down like he was made of butter, and Scat could melt him. The whole time Rao was on the witness stand, Scat had his eyes drilled into that kid's forehead. Rao was squirming bad, sweating up a storm, as he drank glass after glass of water. And if that bastard wasn't going to spend a single day in jail because his father was a detective, at least he was having the worst day of his life right in front of me.

The toughest time I had during the trial was when the city called an engineer from Louisville Slugger, the company that made the aluminum RESPONSE bat, as an expert witness.

"You can see from this demonstration video how a

baseball loses its perfectly rounded shape and compress-
es as it comes in contact with the barrel of the bat," she
testified. "There can be up to eight thousand three hundred pounds of force delivered on impact."

I watched the face of that baseball nearly go flat like a
pancake for a half second in slow motion.

"Oh, God!"

"Lord, no!"

I could hear Mom's and Grandma's cries cutting
through the rest of them in that courtroom.

And the anger just rose up stronger through every
part of me.

SURPRISING WELCOME IN HILLSBORO
—From *The Morning Star Herald*

An African American male from out of state stopped
his car in front of Mario's Pizza in the heart of Hillsboro. Within moments, 39-year-old Monte Larson was
mobbed by a group of white teens. Only on this occa-
sion, they wanted their picture taken with him, as the
residents of this nearly all-white community attempt to
shed their racist image.

"We love black people here," said a teenage male,
who put his arm around Larson's shoulder. "This is the

best pizza and calzone in town. Come inside and we'll get you a table."

Larson, who was traveling north to begin a new job, knew nothing about the ongoing hate-crime trial, in which Noah Jackson, an African American teen from East Franklin, was beaten on the streets of Hillsboro with an aluminum baseball bat more than four months ago. Nor did he know that nearly two decades prior to that incident an African American man was chased into traffic by a mob of white teens before being struck and killed by a car.

"That would be surprising to me by the way I'm being treated now," said Larson, after being informed of those events by our reporter, who was in Hillsboro to do a story on that community's legacy of violence. "I've encountered that kind of hatred before, and this isn't it. But I don't want to be too naïve, either."

According to the latest census, Hillsboro, which is comprised of some 25,000 residents living in mostly single-family homes, is 98 percent white. Neighboring East Franklin, which is eight square miles smaller, has a population of almost 40,000 living for the most part in multifamily apartment complexes. The vast majority (86 percent) of East Franklin residents are African American.

"It's the media that's given us this label. See? Look at how this man's getting treated. We don't have any-thing against these people," said a woman, who de-clined to give her name, as she stepped out of a store to observe the scene. "If my daughter brings one home to marry, so be it."

Chapter **ELEVEN**

CHARLIE SCAT NEVER TOOK THE WITNESS stand.

Instead, he kept his fat ass glued to a chair.

By the second day of the trial, Scat had picked up a pen and started scribbling on a long yellow pad while the lawyers and witnesses talked. I'd follow his hand, and sometimes, it didn't even look like words he was writing.

Maybe that dunce was drawing pictures or doodling.

I would have paid money to be looking over his shoulder and see what was running through his sick mind. But he tore out every paper when he was finished. Then he'd fold it over and bury it deep in the pocket of his blazer.

"He's not even getting up there to defend himself," Dad told me one night while we were playing dominoes in our living room. "That's because he's got no defense. His side's just praying one of them white jurors from Hillsboro is gonna tow that racial line and vote not guilty, no matter what comes out in court."

"I heard justice is supposed to be blind, like the statue of that lady with the scales in her hand outside the court-house," I said snide, playing another tile.

"But people ain't," Dad said, locking the game at both ends and showing me that he was holding the double-blank to win. "And some of them especially ain't *color-blind*.

"Remember that boy they killed in Mississippi back in the fifties—Emmett Till?" Grandma asked Dad, shifting her eyes to me.

"Sure do," answered my father, shuffling the dominoes for another game.

"Nobody can forget!" hollered Mom from the kitchen.

"They murdered him for whistlin' at a white woman, then sunk his body in the river," Grandma went on, laying her sewing down on the table. "The law put the killers who did it on trial. But they sat in court smoking cigarettes, calm as a Sunday picnic, because they knew a white jury from their town would never convict them."

"I heard about that in Mr. Dowling's class," I said, pulling seven new tiles towards me.

"After the killers got off, Emmett's mother made sure the funeral had an open casket," Mom said, as she walked into the living room, wiping her hands on her apron. "That way nobody could be blind to the way he looked after that vicious beating, and soaking in the river for days."

And I thought about those pictures the detectives took of me in the hospital.

My lawyers said that Aaron Chapman would never put Charlie Scat on the stand because he could blow up like a volcano and lose his temper at any minute. They said he'd already cursed at a judge when he didn't get any bail.

But I didn't have to see him on any witness stand to know everything about that pork chop. I just hoped the jury could see it, too. And that none of the white ones from Hillsboro would be blind to it on purpose.

Then the day before the trial ended, the judge gave the boot to a white woman juror after a newspaper printed a story about how she'd once worked at the same job with Scat's uncle.

"I believe that could possibly sway your objectivity," the judge told her in court before replacing her with the first alternate juror—a black dude with gray hair, who looked old enough to be my grandpa.

On the last day of the trial, Aaron Chapman put on a real sideshow, giving his closing speech to the jury.

"Baseball was meant to be a game—something to teach good values," Chapman said, swinging an invisible bat. "There are other games that we learn to play from the time we're very young, and many of those games and *their* values are reinforced by our communities.

"My client, Charles Scaturro, learned that a man *protects* his friends and his neighborhood. That's exactly what he was doing on the night in question—trying to prove himself a man.

"His so-called friends, Rao and Spenelli, came to him upset and feeling threatened by strangers. They came to Charles Scaturro because they felt safe in his presence. They came to him because he'd learned to play the 'protector' game. A game he maybe learned to play too well.

"Now I'll tell you his actions were justified that night. But if you can't agree with me, I'd like you to embrace this thought: Charles Scaturro was in protection mode when he encountered those criminals on the streets of Hillsboro. Not attack mode. Charles Scaturro was doing what teenagers do naturally. He was acting out of passion, playing the cowboy sheriff, if you will. And yes, maybe taking too much authority into his own hands.

"This was not a hate crime. Noah Jackson and his fellow car thieves or gold-chain hoodlums, however you want to view them, just happened to be black.

"And as for that racial slur—the n-word. That's a current *hip-hop* greeting. My client's been inundated by it through movies, TV, and music. So blame Hollywood or the FCC for any cultural misunderstanding he may have possessed.

"Now I want to ask you all to be honest with your-selves. Who here hasn't heard teenage African Americans call each other the n-word? Not in malice. But in friend-ship. And how many of you who disagree with that usage of the word ever stopped to challenge them on it? How many of you here, black or white, have used that word yourself? And none of you have ever perpetrated a hate crime, have you? So don't be a hypocrite and say that it proves something.

"If you must find Charles Scaturro guilty, don't say it was a hate crime. Thank you."

Then the judge gave the jury their instructions, ex-plaining the law to them.

"If you conclude that the defendant did not know that the young men he encountered were there to steal a car, and solely accosted them because of their race, then by law you must find Charles Scaturro guilty of a hate crime."

I watched the jury file out past the stars and stripes on the U.S. flag to their meeting room. Blacks outnum-bered whites two to one. But that didn't matter. The vote had to be unanimous in a criminal case, twelve to zero. And from what I knew about growing up in East Franklin and going to school at Carver High, I didn't believe for a second that there wasn't at least one die-hard cracker in that group of four white jurors who wished he'd been the one to beat me with that bat.

The officers cuffed Charlie Scat and took him away to some cage.

There were reporters on the steps of the courthouse. The city lawyers told me not to talk to them until a verdict came back.

I didn't have anything to say yet anyway.

But Chapman was flapping his gums to a whole crowd of reporters.

"Like I clearly said in court, my client has no ill feelings towards anyone. He's just for keeping his neighborhood safe," he said.

"I hate that man," I told Dad on the low. "I'd like to boot his ass down every one of these stairs."

"You and me both," replied Dad.

It was freezing outside, and the same smoke coming out of Chapman's mouth was pouring from mine.

Two days later, on a Saturday night, I got a call from the city's lawyers telling me not to go to school on Monday morning because the jury had come to a verdict. I'd already missed four days of classes the week before. But I was up on my studying and knew I wouldn't fall into any deep holes over it.

"It's usually good news when they decide so fast," Mom said.

"Yeah, but good for who?" Dad asked, without getting an answer.

On Sunday morning, we took the bus to Centreville.

It was Grandma's idea just to go there and walk.

Most of the stores on Sheffield Street were closed, so we had plenty of sidewalk to ourselves. It was cold and the wind was blowing hard enough that you could hear it. But we were standing in a bright patch of sun.

"Like I said before, it wasn't your time," Grandma told me, looking up at Michael Sheffield's name on the street sign.

"It wasn't your time either, Mama Jackson," Mom said.

I watched the sign shaking in the wind and said, "I just wish I knew what this was all for. Why me?"

"Those are answers we don't have yet, Noah," answered Grandma. "And maybe we wouldn't even understand them if we did."

"Just mortal man caught up in God's plan," said Dad, with his collar turned up against the wind and his hands deep into the pockets of his coat.

The next day in court, I could see Scat's right leg

shaking underneath the table. I guess he had a lot more to lose than me.

But I couldn't figure out what there was to win.

The judge called the jury inside, and once they were all in their seats he asked, "Madam Forewoman, have the members reached a unanimous verdict?"

"We have, Your Honor," said a pale older white lady, with her cheeks painted red.

"Madame Forewoman, how do you find the defendant, Charles Scaturro, on the charges of robbery and assault as a hate crime?" asked the judge.

The woman stood up and cleared her throat.

"Guilty," she said, clear and strong.

The lawyers next to me were slapping my back.

I let out a long breath. But I couldn't find any real reason to celebrate.

Scaturro's sentencing wasn't for another four weeks—a few days after graduation. The city's lawyers needed me to speak at the sentencing, to say why Scaturro should get the whole twenty-five years the judge could give him by law.

So it wasn't over for me.

And nearly every free second I had, that speech was turning over in my mind.

"You got an idea of what it's gonna sound like?" Dad would ask.

But I'd just shake him off and say, "I'm still trying to get ahold of it."

For more than a month, Deshawna and me had stopped arguing, probably because I started having more respect for how hard it was to raise a baby, even just part-time. That made things go a lot easier between us. And sometimes when her and Destiny Love were smiling at the same time, I felt like I wanted Deshawna to be more than just my girlfriend. So for Christmas I bought her a bracelet with lots of little charms that said things like "Boo" and "Super Mom."

On Christmas Day, I watched Destiny Love sitting under the tree at our house, pushing three different kinds of Play-Doh together till it made a brand-new color I'd never seen before.

Then I came home from work one night, just before New Year's Eve, and our apartment was empty when it shouldn't have been. I went to the refrigerator for something to eat and tried to push the idea that anything was wrong out of my head.

But a streak of cold ran through me, and I couldn't touch a bite.

I'd forgot to turn my cell phone back on after work,

and when I did, I saw all the missed calls.

That's when Mom came through the front door with tears in her eyes.

She stood straight in front of me, trembling to get out what she had to say.

"Noah, something terrible—" she said, stopping to take a deep breath.

And I already knew in my heart that Grandma had died.

CORDELL'S FUNERAL HOME—EAST FRANKLIN

The day before Alethea Jackson's wake. Noah and his father sit alone in a side room, waiting to make some of the final arrangements with the funeral director.

DAD: I'll tell you true, it comes in stages, son. (*Looks at the dark wood paneling on the wall.*)

NOAH: What does?

DAD (*Turns his eyes back to Noah.*): Figuring out what it means to be a man. I'm almost forty-six years old now, and it still keeps changing. First, I thought I was a man when I was old enough to shave. Then once I got married and made a baby, I thought that was it.

NOAH: It wasn't?

DAD: When my father passed, I thought for sure I knew, because I was the man of the house then. But I'll tell you what I've learned now—it's not till both your parents are gone and leave you here all alone on this earth that you really know what it is.

NOAH: Let me hear.

DAD: They've left, and it's your turn. You need to make sure your children know how to stand on their own two feet. That you've taught them something better than what you knew to start out. And that they're always the most important thing, because this is gonna be their world soon, not yours. That's what it is, Noah. Don't let the bullshit that comes flying at you every day get your mind fixed on anything else.

NOAH: I'll keep watch for it. I promise.

DAD: Keeping watch isn't enough, 'cause your eyes can fool you. Like they did when that car you went to steal looked more valuable than everything your family ever taught you.

NOAH: I guess it takes some smarts, too.

DAD: It's called maturity, son. Hopefully, from everything you been through, you're beginning to get some.

Chapter TWELVE

AT GRANDMA'S WAKE, DESTINY LOVE WAS saying, "Gam-Gam" and reaching out for her in the casket, like she hadn't really left us.

There was a bulletin board up front by where Grandma was resting, with pictures of her and my grandpa, who died the day before I turned two years old. And there was even a big sunflower pinned to it, because that's where she was born—Sunflower, Mississippi.

The funeral home was packed with people from all over our neighborhood who'd come to pay their respects. Lots of older people get cranky and spend half their time lecturing everybody, telling them how it should be. But even when I heard Grandma scold folks for playing their music too loud or leaving the covers off the trash cans in front of our building, they didn't get mad at her. And Grandma usually wound up pulling them in closer.

"She could spank you hard with one hand and hug with the other at the same time," Dad said, proud. "This turnout's a tribute to her character."

My parents were both acting strong.

It was Deshawna who was a wreck, and she couldn't even look at the casket.

"That's 'cause she lost her own mother so young," Mom told me. "You're gonna have to put some of your own grief aside and be there for her, Noah."

So I tried the best that I could.

Part of me felt empty, and I wanted to break down bawling right there.

But the rest of me knew that Grandma didn't get cheated out of a thing in her life, and lived it to the fullest.

And I wasn't sure how, but I wanted to live the same way.

Then Mr. Dowling walked through the door and my heart jumped up a little.

As he walked over to my family, I noticed he had an envelope in his hand.

"I'm sorry for your great loss, Mr. and Mrs. Jackson, Noah," he said, shaking Mom's and Dad's hands first, then mine.

That's when I saw Hendricks's name on the outside of that envelope, and realized it was the letter that Grandma had me deliver to him at school.

"Mr. Hendricks asked that I return this to your family," he told us, handing the envelope to Dad. "I can tell you that he was truly saddened to hear the news of your mother's passing. She must have made a real impression on him. He even debated coming here with me to pay his respects, but I guess he didn't want to intrude."

"So he sent back this letter from her, instead?" Mom asked, puzzled, as Dad took it out of the envelope, and they both read it.

"Said he felt like he needed to share this with you all," Mr. Dowling said, lifting his own shoulders. "I haven't looked at it."

I wanted to read that letter bad, but not in a crowd of eyes.

I wanted a chance at it alone.

"Yeah, that's the best of her, right there," Dad said after he'd finished. "I'm not surprised she could touch a hardened man like that."

And Mom agreed.

I reached my hand out and Dad gave me the letter.

Then I walked off to read it, with Grandma resting just a few feet away.

Mr. Hendricks—

I praise God for working His will through you.

No matter how different we are, we were both made by the same hand.

That makes us all brothers and sisters.

So brother, I say to you—Thank you.

Thank you for the gift of a new day with my family.

You are a teacher as I hope to be.

Teach me and I will try to teach you.

With God's grace we will learn together.

—Alethea Jackson

The feeling in Grandma's letter stayed with me as I studied for my final exams.

Even with the pressure of everything going on in my life, I passed them all.

In the end, just nineteen out of forty "super seniors" graduated with me in January. I guess the other twenty-one didn't have the support I did, and found a way to fail a class.

The graduation ceremony was small enough to hold in the school's library.

I sat there in my purple cap and gown, looking at those thousands of books on the shelves. That got me thinking about all those people from history who had something so important to say they needed to write it down for somebody to read.

I still didn't know what I was going to say at Scat's sentencing.

Was it really going to mean anything—to me or anybody else?

Was it my turn to beat up on him, or could I be somebody better?

The principal called my name. "Noah Jackson."

I walked across the floor in front of Mom, Dad, my daughter, and the rest of the parents, to get my diploma. There was an extra cheer for me from everybody, no matter what color they were.

Lots of the senior teachers were there, including Mr. Dowling.

The only important teacher I had who was missing was Grandma.

When the ceremony was over, all of the graduates tossed their caps up to the ceiling.

Mom was holding Destiny Love, and she put her into my arms for a picture. I wanted Deshawna to be there, too, but she was taking her GED exam that day.

"Smile, little girl. Your daddy's an official high-school graduate," Mom said. "Soon to be college student, and one day—engineer."

"We're not talking about an engineer on a train anymore," said Dad. "No, sir. There are bigger things waitin' for my son in college."

If it wasn't for that talk I'd had with Dad before Grandma's wake, I would have sworn that holding my baby and a diploma made me a man.

At Scat's sentencing, I sat in the courtroom listening to the city's lawyers make their case why the judge should give him the max—twenty-five years in prison. I glanced over at Scat, trying to figure out what he'd look like at forty-something, when he'd be released. But no matter how much I tried in my mind, his face wouldn't change for me.

When the city's lawyers finished, they told the judge that I wanted to speak.

They'd phoned me twice that week wanting to know what I was going to say, and even offered to help me write it. But it all felt too private, and I wouldn't let them hear a word in advance. Anyway, I'd kept changing it, right up until the night before.

I walked to the courtroom's wooden podium, where the lawyers usually spoke from, and pulled the white sheet of paper from the inside pocket of my suit jacket. Then I unfolded it, smoothing it out on the flat surface in front of me.

I filled my lungs with air and found my voice.

"When my friends and myself went into Hillsboro that night, I had the wrong thing on my mind. Wanting to steal a car was a bad idea, and I take responsibility for that. I have nobody to blame for that mistake but me," I said, turning my eyes towards Scat. "But what you did that night changed my life. At first, it made me start to hate all white people. I felt like every one of them wanted my blood if they ever saw me outside of East Franklin.

"But I was lucky. I'm not completely ignorant like you. I had people in my life, like my parents and my grandmother, to help me see things clearer and learn that life isn't about that. So I have overcome those feelings of racial hatred.

"I was also bitter about why this all happened to me. But now I see everything that I learned from this, and how it helped me to look at my life and appreciate all my blessings.

"Because of your hatred and ignorance, I could have been killed. Then you would have robbed my baby daughter of her father, hurting two generations of black people with one swing of a baseball bat. You need to study your actions, and ask yourself if you really hate her, too.

"I don't know how much time the judge should give you. That's not my job. That's not why I was put on this earth.

"Right now, I'm a son and a father, and one day I hope to look at myself as a man.

"Part of me understands your hatred, because I've felt it, too. I only hope that you can learn from your actions, take responsibility for them, and after you've paid for what you did—change.

"That's all I want to happen. I'm done."

I folded the paper over twice, putting it back into my pocket.

Then I stepped away from the podium feeling satisfied with my response, like I'd put some huge mountain I never thought I could climb behind me. And as I walked back to my seat, I could see by the proud look on my father's face that maybe he thought I'd done that, too.

When the judge called on Charlie Scat to speak, he stood up at the defendant's table with his hands behind his back, even though he wasn't cuffed.

"I'm just like Noah Jackson—only opposite. I can't trust black people now. They all look at me like I'm a racist, and like they might want to hurt me because of this case. And that's not who I really am. That's just the way the district attorney wants people to see me—like I'm some kind of terrible monster," said Scat, off the top of his head.

Then he opened a piece of paper and started to read from it.

"I am responsible for my actions. One hundred percent responsible. I want to apologize to Noah Jackson. I want to apologize to his family, too, because I know how much this incident has hurt my own. My mother couldn't even be here today because it hurts her so much to see this happening to her son. So from the very bottom of my heart, I'd like to say I'm sorry. But this was not a hate crime. This had nothing to do with Noah Jackson being black. It never did. This was about me trying to protect friends—false friends. This was about me protecting my neighborhood and making a stupid mistake. The jury didn't see that because the DA told them I was a demon. And they bought it. But I'm hoping that you—Your Honor, with your legal experience—won't be fooled like that."

Then Scat sat back down, and the only sound in the courtroom was from the reporters in the back row writing the last of his words.

The judge put on his glasses and studied the papers in front of him for a few seconds, before he took them off again to speak.

"It's plain for me to see that this defendant lacks good judgment, moral character, and any true comprehension of remorse. I find the defendant to be both hateful and brutal in his prior actions. He is truly part of the problem, not only in this city, but also in this country. Nothing in our history has caused more grief and suffering than racism, and the defendant, in my opinion, lives it, breathes it, and if not painted into this corner would continue to preach it. The very nature of his crime amplifies the message of racial intolerance and attempts to drag our society down to its lowest depths. I only hope that he may one day learn better," the judge said, raising his gavel. "With those findings in mind, I hereby sentence Charles Scaturro to eighteen years in the state prison on the charges of robbery and assault as a hate crime."

Scat winced as the *crack* of the judge's gavel ripped through the courtroom, and a big part of it was over for me.

I left there surrounded by my family, knowing I'd have to fight hard every day to get where I wanted to go, and stay focused on who I wanted to be.

I was satisfied that I didn't sink to Scat's level, feeding whatever was left of the negative feelings inside of me.

I didn't even have to make people see who Charlie Scat and the rest of those racists from Hillsboro really were. Scat and his friends did that themselves, with their own words and everything they did. And now there was no way any of them could ever hide it or pretend it wasn't the truth.

Outside, I looked down at the high courthouse steps. I

could see how the smooth stones that formed them were laid together side by side, supporting the weight that none of them could hold alone.

And I wondered, in my whole life, if I'd ever build something like that for people to climb.

TURN THE PAGE TO READ AN EXCERPT
FROM PAUL VOLPONI'S NEXT BOOK

RIKERS HIGH

CHAPTER

1

Every morning at five o'clock another correction officer came on duty and started to count. For five months it had been the same. One of them would drive in from someplace nice, like Long Island, while another went home. The one coming on would start down the row of beds, counting, before he could steal an hour or two of sleep in the Plexiglas bubble—their little command center at the front of our module.

They can't take the count by looking. Just like in the movies, a kid could roll his clothes up under a blanket and be on the loose. So they count by feeling for a warm body.

There's nothing worse than waking up when a CO touches you. For a second, you might not remember where you are. You might even think you're home. Then it all comes rushing back into your brain. You're on Rikers Island. To fall asleep again is like spending another night in jail.

"Thirty-six . . . thirty-seven . . . thirty-eight," the CO muttered.

The new jack next to me had spent the night before fighting off the wolves for his good kicks. He didn't know the routine yet, and wasn't ready for anyone to touch him while he was still asleep.

"Who's that?" he screamed, jumping up in his bed.

"Yo, thirty-nine!" the CO shot back, pinning his shoulders to the mattress. "I'm just takin' the count, kid. Grab a fuckin' hold of yourself!"

It seemed like half the house was awake for a few seconds, until they saw it was nothing.

"Forty, court!" the officer hollered, and shook me with one hand.

I was going to court this morning. I got my best clothes—my cleanest jeans and collared polo shirt—from the plastic bucket under my bed. Then I got dressed in the dark.

I didn't tell anyone I expected to go home. Some inmates will start trouble with you because they're jealous or think you won't fight back and chance getting a new charge. The ones you owe from juggling commissary will want to settle right away. Anyone who owes *you* will put it off, hoping you don't come back from court. And the sneak thieves will be looking for your blanket and what's left of your commissary and clothes before your bed gets cold.

I walked up to the bubble where the COs sit, and I got in line with the other courts. A CO pulled my ID card from the box and threw it on top of the pile of black and brown faces. It read, "Martin Stokes—Adolescent Reception and Detention Center, Mod-3, North Side #40." I had been answering to "Forty" for so long, it was almost like that was really my name. I would only hear "Martin" when I called home, or when Mom came on a visit.

The picture stapled to the corner of the card was taken my first day on the Island, two weeks before I turned seventeen. I thought I'd be here for a hot minute then. It was such a bubble-gum charge. I thought Mom could make my $5,000 bail, or I'd get a program and probation when I got to court. But my case was put off twice for bullshit.

First, my lawyer had to tell the judge we weren't ready. Then the judge got held up on another case. Now it had been five months since I was out in the world, and I was hungry to see it again without peeping through a chain-link fence.

There was a bang at the steel door to our mod.

It was a woman CO who'd come to collect me and four other kids. We eyeballed her up and down. She was pretty enough. But women don't have to look too good in jail to get a lot of attention. Most times, inmates, especially adolescents, are just happy to be anywhere near one. Only I was thinking more about Mom, and getting a chance to see my little sisters, Trisha and Tina, and Grandma again.

We deuced it up in the hall, getting into two lines. That woman CO had inmates from other houses out there, and we were already mixing with adults, who have their own modules.

Then she marched us down the main corridor. Except for other officers standing their posts, it was totally empty. And with the sun coming up behind those barred windows, I started to think about how it's almost peaceful on Rikers that early in the morning, when the only movement through the halls are the courts.

CHAPTER
2

We got to the yard, and I was shackled to another inmate by my foot and wrist, so it would be that much harder for either of us to run. They loaded us onto a blue and white bus with the word CORRECTION painted on the side. Like people on the streets wouldn't figure it out from the metal bars and plates on the windows. Then the bus started up, and we passed through the big gates and over the bridge that separates Rikers Island from the world.

There were fourteen pairs of inmates shackled together and two officers along for the ride. One CO stays with the inmates, and the driver sits on the other side of the bars so no one can take control of the bus. There's even a cage that the CO can lock you up in if you start trouble or need protection. The mood on the way to court is usually pretty good. But the ride back can be long and hard if enough dudes get smacked down by the judges.

We crossed the bridge and were on the streets of East Elmhurst. It felt good to see people walking in any direction they wanted, without a CO to stop them. And I wanted to be that way again, too.

I saw a man picking up after his dog on a corner, and I thought about my first trip to the Island. Maybe I was ten years old then. Mom took me on a visit with her to see Pops on Rikers. But we got off some city bus and couldn't find the jail.

She stopped a white man walking a black Rottweiler and asked, "How do you get to Rikers Island?"

The man just laughed and said, "Rob a bank, lady. Rob a bank."

I know where the Island is *now*. I know the bus route from the jail to the Queens Criminal Courthouse and back. I've taken that ride so many times on this one case, I could close my eyes and tell you where the bus is by the bumps and turns. From the streets to the Grand Central Parkway, through the exit ramp and the turn onto Queens Boulevard, I could feel it in my bones.

At the courthouse, we were put into the pens. You pick up a lot of skills in jail, and in the pens you need them all. The pens are big cells, with maybe fifty inmates inside of each one. That's where everybody waits until their case gets called. There's an open toilet, a sink, and benches bolted to the floor so nobody throws them. The COs in charge aren't interested in what you do because they don't have to live with you for long. They don't really want to come inside and stop anything, either. It's up to you to take care of yourself. As long as you come out in one piece to see the judge, they did their job.

Adolescents are mixed with adults in the pens, and guys that fly the same colors stay together and act tight. By eleven o'clock, the COs serve you a slice of bologna between two pieces of bread for lunch. Inmates call them "cop-out sandwiches" because you'd be willing to confess to anything just to not eat that crap. After a while, the floor of the pen gets covered with bologna and stale bread.

I tried to look hard, with my chest puffed out and eyes squinting. I was as worried about the next few hours as I was about my case.

Some guys had bullied a weak kid over in the corner into doing the pogo—jumping up and down in the toilet on one foot in his shoes and socks. It's mostly the adolescents who do stuff like that because they want to show other kids how tough they are. The only time an adult will step to an adolescent is if the kid is acting real stupid. And when adults fight, there's no playing around. They'll pull burners quick and try to stab each other to death.

The dude standing next to me was practicing hand signs, and I thought he was down with one of the gangs. He saw me watching him and said, "This is what's gonna help me beat my case."

Then he ran down the whole show for me.

"All the judges are Masons," he said. "If they see you throwing up the right signs, they won't find you guilty. That's why you don't see white people going through the system. Most of them are Masons, and they know the signs. But there are black Masons, too. Even a white judge knows that."

I just nodded. You never want to argue with a dude when he has his hopes riding on something crazy like that. Not while he's waiting to see the judge and is all uptight.

There were two kids starting to jaw in the corner of the pen. They were fighting over which outfit ran their neighborhood, and it was starting to get heavy. They both had on their best ice grills, and one of them had backup.

"You're talkin' to me like I'm some sort of punk," said the one standing alone.

He put his fists up and stood with his back to the bars, so no one could yoke him from behind. But that crew had him surrounded and other inmates in that part of the pen started to move away.

It was about to be high drama when an officer came up to the bars and shouted, "All right boys and *girls*, listen up! Fuller, Douglas, Stokes, and Wallace, let's go!"

"That's me, Martin Stokes," I told the officer, as his key rattled the lock on the door.

CHAPTER

I hadn't seen my legal aid lawyer since the last time I went to court, fifty-one days ago. I'd called her plenty since then, and so did Mom. But she was never there and wouldn't get back to us. That happened so many times we got to know the message on her answering machine by heart and would tear it to pieces on visits.

"I'm either in court right now or on the phone. Leave your name and case number, and I'll get back to you as soon as possible."

One time, I just screamed "Forty!" into the phone and hung up.

I'd only met her five minutes before I saw the judge on my first trip to court. Until she said my name, I had no idea she was my lawyer. She was young and black, and I thought she was the girl or sister of somebody on trial. Then I noticed the briefcase in her hand.

"My name is Gale Thompson," she said, inside of a small conference room. "I've been assigned to represent you in this matter."

Before she even asked me what happened, she started to explain how I was guilty and what kind of deal she could get me.

They had me for "steering"—telling an undercover cop where to buy weed in my neighborhood. I told her I did it, but that it was really a setup. How the dude who walked up to me was diesel, and I was afraid not to tell him anything or he might start to beef with me. I told her that she had to tell my side of it, too, before I got anywhere near calling myself guilty.

We argued back and forth for a while. Then she just threw her hands up and sent a note to the judge saying we weren't ready. He didn't like that, and I had to wait almost ten weeks to come back. That's when I thought Mom would do anything to make my bail. But she didn't have the money and had to worry about supporting my sisters and Grandma.

I didn't see Miss Thompson again until the next time my case came up.

"I hope you're through with all that nonsense and we can get down to the business of getting you home," she said. "I've got a lot of cases to handle, and this one is cut and dry."

By then I'd seen lots of kids go home on more serious charges. I just wanted to be done with jail and to get my ass out of this stinking parade. So I kept my mouth shut. But the judge got caught up in some case that went to trial, and I never even made it into the courtroom that day.

Now I was glad to see Miss Thompson. I was happy to get out of the pen before it exploded and finally go home. The CO took me to a side room where she was sitting at a table, studying her papers.

"I've arranged for you to go home and get off this public support." she said. "The assistant DA has agreed to probation, but the judge is out sick and we have to come back in a couple of weeks, on the nineteenth."

My brain just shut down for a second, and it was like I was frozen stiff.

I couldn't believe it. I was going back to Rikers Island.

Couldn't they get another judge? Couldn't the DA just send me home?

I was tired of getting shuffled around, and she was the only one in the room to hear it. So I started to bark at her.

"This is 'cause of you, right? 'Cause you're a miserable shit lawyer!"

Miss Thompson took a deep breath.

"I saw your mother in the courtroom," she said, in an even tone. "I gave her the news, and she was very upset. I tried my best to calm her down and let her know I have a handle on it—that you'll be home soon."

But I wouldn't cut her an inch of slack, and stared her down.

Miss Thompson stood up and started stuffing papers into her briefcase.

"Oh, yeah, and thanks for all those times you never picked up the phone or called my mother back!"

"I don't like the system much either, Martin. The truth is, you get what you pay for," she popped off. "The city picks up this bill. I represent over fifty clients like you at the same time, *all* brothers or Hispanics. It's delicatessen-style justice in here. Take a number and wait. That's how it works."

Then Miss Thompson walked out the door and the CO came back inside to get me.

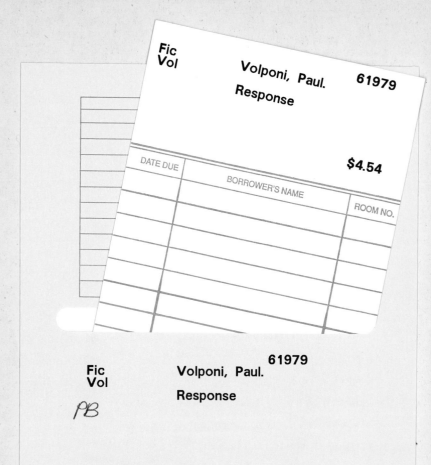